CUT TO RIBBONS

Hundreds of iciclelike shards littered the rug. It was as though a tornado had flown in through the window and randomly trashed every picture in the place.

This was no normal break-in.

I bent down and picked up a broken frame. And froze. Because Rich looked back at me from a blowup of a photo I remembered. Knife slashes mutilated his face.

Was this Dot's handiwork? A woman gone over the brink, so consumed with jealousy and rage she had desecrated her own home?

My legs almost gave out when I saw blood on the picture. For one moment of dementia, I thought the picture was bleeding. Then I realized the blood must be coming from my own hand. . . .

PINK
BALLOONS

AND
OTHER
DEADLY
THINGS

A MYSTERY NOVEL

NANCY TESLER

A DELL BOOK

Published by

DELL PUBLISHING

a division of

BANTAM DOUBLEDAY DELL PUBLISHING GROUP, INC.

1540 Broadway

New York, New York 10036

ISBN: 0-440-22406-3

Printed in the United States of America

Published simultaneously in Canada

June 1997

10 9 8 7 6 5 4 3 2 1

RAD

This book is dedicated with love to
Ann Loring
insightful mentor and rare friend,
whose unflagging faith and encouragement through
the worst of times and the best of times kept this
writer writing.

Acknowledgments

My heartfelt thanks and gratitude go to my exceptional agent, Grace Morgan, for guiding and believing in me, to Jackie Farber, my estimable and discerning editor, and to her indefatigable assistant, Lisa Lustgarten, all of whom have made this experience such a positive one.

To my friend and fellow author David Beckman, for the use of his wonderful poem, "Over," my deepest appreciation.

Thanks also to the friends and professional colleagues whose input and support were invaluable: biofeedback therapist Patricia Spiech, Dr. Mary Jo Sabo, Leah Gabriel, Amy Miale, Dr. Gail Haft, and all the "knights and ladies of the pen" of the Friday evening "round" table.

Last, but definitely not least, very special thanks to Mike Friedman and to my sons, Ken, Bob, and Doug, for their love.

SATURDAY
MAY 22

AFTERWARD I WOULD
blame myself for having missed the warning signs. Among
my colleagues I have a reputation for being intuitive.
Probably I was too close to the situation. Couldn't see the
sky for the storm clouds.

Or the killer for the smoke in my eyes.

My name is Caroline Carlin Burnham, Carrie to my

friends, Ms. Carlin to my clients at the biofeedback center, Cat to my husband, Rich. But that was when we were together, and pet names were a sign of his affection. In the early days of our marriage, it was Kitten. At the end it was Nudnik. (Translated, that's nag, nuisance, and all-round pain in the ass.). Definitely no affection intended. If he has a name for me now, I don't want to know what it is.

Adding insult to the agony of my impending divorce, last Saturday I turned forty. A double whammy.

Chances are none of it would have happened if it hadn't been for the heat wave. Certainly not in the way it did, anyway. The thermometer outside my window had soared to ninety degrees for four days running. My office, which is in one of those buildings with a sensational view of the Hudson from hermetically sealed picture windows, and without air conditioning till June, could have doubled for a sauna.

When my three o'clock canceled at the last minute, I had the computer switched off before it had spewed the final session printout. I flew out of the building, got in my '89 Honda, blasted the air conditioning in my face, and gave my trusty steed its head. Was it my fault it aimed straight for the street it used to call home?

Don't ask me what it was that day that impelled me to drive past my old house. I thought I'd worked through the worst of the jealous crazies. Maybe the heat had gotten to me and affected my judgment. Maybe it was hearing about the wedding plans.

Or maybe it was the dream.

I am barefoot on wet tile, staring at a giant beach ball leaking port-wine splotches, staining the snowy tiles as it bounces alongside a pool. I watch as it slips over the edge, glances off a body floating face-down, a ribbon trailing from the blood-caked, mud-caked tangled mass of hair. Red. Like the water. I scream, but there is no sound, only the lap . . . lap . . . lap of the water as it sloshes against the aquamarine wall.

She was poolside, lolling on my favorite chaise longue, wearing only the bottom half of a bikini. The suit's stark whiteness set off the bronze of her oh-so-smoothly-tanned skin. Her honey-blond hair was plaited into a heavy braid and encircled her head like a misplaced halo.

From where I'd parked in my ex–next door neighbor's driveway, I could see without being seen.

A phone rang, and I watched as she lazily extended one graceful arm and plucked the receiver from its cradle. My sixth sense was working overtime. I knew who was on the line. Her shrill laughter carried across the manicured lawn, catapulting me from the car as though I'd been ejected from a jet plane.

Like a burglar casing his next hit, I skulked along the overgrown bushes that separate our raised ranch from the Millers' colonial, suppressing a wail of protest as I recognized the antique gold chain nestled between those curvaceous twenty-eight-year-old breasts. Its diamond and ruby clasp glittered and sparkled in the sunlight.

Phone tucked under her chin, she unscrewed the cap

on a bottle of nail polish and began applying appropriately scarlet paint to her talons.

". . . just back from Bergdorf's," she was saying. "Anything fabulous'll run about five." A pause, then a giggle. "Thousand, you dinosaur. And don't tell me you can't afford it! I'm your marketing director, remember? Shit!"

She made a grab for the bottle as it toppled from its perch between the heaving mounds, leaving a crimson trail across her bra-line-free shoulders.

" 'S what bridal gowns run nowadays. You want me looking drop-dead gorgeous, you're gonna have to live with the price tag."

Our divorce wasn't even final. The body wasn't cold, and they were planning the wedding!

She gave a throaty laugh. "Well, I'm a little smarter than *she* was."

Oh, Erica Vogel, you are a lot smarter. You have Rich Burnham paying five thousand dollars for a wedding dress. Mine had cost five hundred. That was eighteen years ago, and it'd never occurred to me that I shouldn't pay for it myself. I started calculating how many hours I'd have to work for five thousand dollars. Matt could go to soccer camp for two summers for five thousand dollars! Allie could take singing lessons forever. The top of my head felt like a pressure cooker about to blow. If the gown cost that much, how much was Rich forking out for the wedding? And at the Waldorf, yet.

I was about to find out. Tiptoeing from behind a row of pine trees, I made it to the protective branches of the giant weeping willow I'd planted as a sprout fourteen years earlier.

". . . haggling with the banquet manager," she was saying as she mopped at the congealing polish. "November's the earliest date I could get. Figure around two, two-fifty a person, not counting the flowers and the band. And the invitations and the photographer, of course. So if we don't invite more than a couple of hundred . . ."

The pressure cooker exploded into hiccoughs. I clapped my hands over my mouth to muffle the sound and sank to the ground, oblivious to the pebbles and brambles that scraped my legs. Frantically I mumbled my mantra. "I'm calm, this is not a life-threatening situation. . . ."

Erica frowned, glanced in my direction, but went on painting. The sharp edge of a toy boomerang half buried in the loose soil cut into my ankle. I shoved it aside, barely feeling the sting.

Her voice became syrupy, but the expression on her face said something quite different as she swung one foot and viciously kicked Matt's favorite soccer ball into the mucky half-filled pool.

"Whatever you think, honey. Twelve's a little old for a flower girl, but if you really want Allie in the wedding party—"

Over my dead body! Better yet, over hers! My hand found a rock. Stoning. That was it. The punishment for adultery in the Old Testament. To hell with that turning-the-other-cheek stuff they're pushing in the new one.

" 'Course," she snickered, "the dragon lady might have something to say about that."

The "dragon lady" certainly would. My daughter would be her flower girl the day flowers grew on glaciers.

I'd heard all I could stand. I had to get out of there before I grabbed that nail polish and smeared a gigantic A across those perfect boobs.

I scrambled to my feet and sneaked out of the yard. My imagination went into orbit. Stoning was too kind. Strangling, decapitation—those had potential. I envisioned myself twisting that chain around her slender throat, hurling Matt's boomerang across the yard, severing the Aryan head from its willowy neck. I pictured the bleached braid hanging on my belt, stretched her on a Spanish Inquisition rack. I burned her at a stake in Salem. Wait. First I wanted her pilloried, with the whole town throwing rotten fruit in her face. Then I'd stone, strangle, and rack her.

I dashed across the Millers' lawn to my car, nearly mowing down Sue Tomkins, who was walking her Yorkie.

"Carrie? That you?"

Mumbling an apology, I jerked open my car door, jumped in, turned the key, and roared off, leaving Sue standing openmouthed, the yapping Yorkie straining at its leash. By morning the whole town of Alpine would be buzzing. Maybe all of Bergen County. I didn't care. I was plotting my revenge.

I didn't hear the siren until flashing lights appeared in my rearview mirror. Coasting to a stop, I waited for the unmarked brown car to swerve past. It didn't.

The gaunt craggy-featured man who unfolded himself

from behind the wheel wasn't wearing a uniform, and briefly I toyed with the idea of flooring the accelerator in the hope he might be a carjacker instead of a cop. Except no self-respecting carjacker would risk his freedom for a six-and-a-half-year-old Honda. I took a deep breath, rolled down my window, and raised my red-rimmed eyes to his cool slate ones.

He flashed a badge. "May I see your license and registration, please?"

I fumbled around in my bag for my wallet, reached into the glove compartment, handed him the documents.

"You live in the next town, Mrs. Burnham," he said, his voice tight with disapproval. "You must know this is a school zone. You were doing forty-five in a twenty-five-mile zone."

I muttered something about not realizing I was going so fast—I'd had a lot on my mind. And prayed, because I sure as hell couldn't afford a speeding ticket, with its accompanying points and surcharges.

God must've had a free minute, or maybe plainclothes cops don't issue tickets, because he handed me back my papers.

"Try not to let it affect your driving," he said, and strolled back to his car.

Two minutes of diaphragmatic breathing, and my heart rate returned to normal. I was getting ready to start the engine when the phone rang.

My blood pressure zoomed. I don't give this number to anyone but my children, and they have strict instructions not to call unless, at the very least, they're hooked up to an IV in a hospital emergency room.

"Hello."

"Mom?"

"What happened? What's the matter?"

"There's a lady real upset, wants to know can you see her tomorrow."

I turned up the air conditioning, letting the cool air whip across my face. "Allie," I scolded, "couldn't this have waited till I got home?"

"But—she says she's having a crisis."

The distress in my child's voice brought me up short. "Sorry, honey, I'm a little uptight. I nearly got a ticket. Put me on hold and ask who it is."

I'm a biofeedback clinician with a new, not-very-large private practice. Before my separation I worked for a pain clinic. Part of my job involved teaching people how to control their internal responses to pain and stress through relaxation training. It's a kind of "heal thyself" alternative to the conventional medical approach. When Rich defected, everyone at the center was sympathetic, but it soon became apparent that a practitioner who'd temporarily lost the ability to practice what she preached was setting a lousy example. I quit before they fired me, went into therapy, got my head together, relatively speaking, and ultimately started my own practice.

My fingers drummed impatiently on the dashboard as I reviewed the possibilities. Who could be so upset as to need to see me on a weekend? Maybe, I worried, Ruth-Ann had had another abreaction, or Phyllis had worked herself up into a migraine again. It's rare for me to get an emergency call, though. Except for my ADD (Attention Deficit Disorder) kids, the bulk of my practice consists of people with anxiety-related diseases, but I'm not an M.D., and most of my patients continue to see their own doctor or therapist.

Allie came back on the line.

"It's Vickie. She says her doctor's away."

Victoria Thorenson, a relatively new patient, the one who had canceled today's session. Not yet twenty, with pixie good looks, Vickie should have been on the threshold of a wonderful life, but she lives on an emotional trampoline, bouncing from one man to another. According to her psychiatrist, she had a history of involvements with unavailable men, setting herself up for failure. The affair with the latest lasted for over a year, but recently he broke it off. I had just switched her from breathing and relaxation exercises to guided visualizations, where she'd been picturing herself as successful and independent. Normally an easy visualizer, that one had been giving her trouble.

I sighed. "Tell her I'll see her at noon."

" 'Kay."

"Maybe we'll send out for pizza tonight."

"Fantabulous!"

It's not hard to make a twelve-year-old's day.

I replaced the phone in its niche and sat there thinking about how my Sunday was getting shot to hell. Ruth-Ann, one of my overeaters, was coming for a session at eleven. She's an Orthodox Jew, so I make an exception and see her on Sundays. And now I had Vickie at twelve, which meant I wouldn't get home till nearly one-thirty. That left less than half a day with the kids.

I sat there letting the air conditioning blow its stale breath in my face, love-hating Rich, wondering if he ever worried about the effect of our impending divorce on Matt and Allie, if he ever had regrets. Did he remember how crazily we had once loved each other, or had his passion for Erica erased the memories from the blackboard of his mind like yesterday's homework assignment?

And then, as always, the nagging voice that wouldn't be stilled—had I, in some way I hadn't realized, been responsible? Maybe I should have studied the stock market, learned about mergers and acquisitions. Maybe I should've worn sexier underwear, watched porn flicks with him, had a breast augmentation. Maybe dinner every night with the children had been too much strain. Maybe I should have fed them early and served him gourmet dinners, followed by orgasms on and under the table.

A car screeched around the corner, bringing me back to reality. All I'd need to complete my day would be to have Rich see me loitering in the neighborhood as he drove home to his lady love.

I switched on the ignition. No response. I tried again. A feeble clunk, then nothing. With rising agitation and a sinking heart, it began to penetrate—what I'd done. Run the air conditioner without the motor on. All my murderous thoughts that day, and the only thing I'd managed to kill was my own DieHard battery!

SUNDAY
MAY 23

The body shudders, starts to roll over, and . . .

I AWOKE FLAILING WILDLY, knocking Luciano and Placido into each other, resulting in a howling, spitting feline cacophony that would have left their namesakes hoarse for a month. My hands felt wet, and I pulled them out from beneath the comforter, half expecting to see blood. Damp with perspiration, they were still trembling, but they were clean.

There was a tentative knock. "Mom?"

Reaching for my robe, I made an effort to sound normal. "Come on in, Matt."

The ten-year-old male love of my life bounced into my room.

"You were makin' noises? You sick?"

I held out my arms. "Bad dream. C'mere."

He took a flying leap across the room and landed next to me. I wrapped my arms around him. Matt's a cuddler. I'm enjoying it for as long as it lasts. I figured I've got two more years of hugs at most till the testosterone kicks in and Mom becomes passé.

"Allie says we can't go on the picnic today."

I'd forgotten all about the afternoon we'd planned at Sterling Forest. "Oh, puss, I'm sorry. I have to work."

He pulled away. "It's Sunday. You said you'd be finished by noon."

I love my work, but for just a fleeting moment, I envied the fifties mom who could stay home with her children.

"I can't help it, Matt. The lady who called yesterday has an emergency."

"You're not a doctor."

He had a point. Besides which, at this particular time in my life, I don't think I'm the best person to work with Vickie. I have a problem relating to "other woman" types. Especially young ones.

"Could we go for a swim at home"—embarrassed, he corrected himself—"I mean, at Dad's then? I know it's not our weekend with him, but it's so hot."

I waited for the pain in my gut to subside. Despite my

months of therapy, the image of my children frolicking in our swimming pool with their father's Playboy bunny was enough to incite me to acts of violence. When I could unclench my teeth, I waffled, "I don't think the pool's been cleaned and filled yet, sweetheart. It's only May."

He turned his back on me. "Aw, man, that sucks!"

I didn't think this was the time for a lecture on the unpleasant connotation of certain words. "I don't even have my car, honey. I had to take a cab home yesterday."

The back remained unyielding.

"Maybe you and Allie could rent a movie," I ventured. "When I get home, we'll grill out. It'll be kind of like a picnic."

He was silent for a moment, then he turned back and snuggled up. "Okay."

I sighed, relieved. He was all right. I lay there, stroking his silky hair, allowing his presence to warm me while I listened to him prattle on about how his Little League coach thought he should try playing catcher, and I shouldn't worry because he would always be wearing a catcher's mask and knee guards and a guard for his other vulnerable parts.

I put the dream out of my mind.

LUGGING A SMALL fan, I took an un-air-conditioned bus to my office, which is in Piermont, New York, just across the New Jersey border. Because of the Sunday bus schedule, what is normally only a fifteen-minute drive from my Norwood, New Jersey, home, took almost an hour. By the time I arrived, at about ten-thirty, I was already out of sorts from the heat and the inconvenience. It didn't help my disposition when I had to spend the next twenty minutes on the phone trying to find a garage that would rescue my abandoned vehicle on a Sunday.

Ruth-Ann was late, so after I slid her disk into the computer and pulled up her protocol, I took the opportunity to open the mail I'd ignored yesterday, hoping for some checks. I switched on the radio, letting the music wash over me as I flipped through the pile of advertisements. Some corner of my mind noted when the news came on, but nothing registered until I heard the words, ". . . affluent community of Alpine."

". . . early this morning," the announcer was saying, "the semi-nude body was discovered by her fiancé. The victim has been identified as twenty-eight-year-old Erica Vogel of . . ."

My pencil and two nails broke simultaneously.

". . . employed by Mr. Burnham for the past three years. The police are not commenting, but it is believed foul play has not been ruled . . ."

I didn't hear a word after "foul play." If I hadn't been dripping already, I'd have broken out in a cold sweat. The pencil dropped from my hand. I began hyperventilating, like the time I took a soccer ball in the gut playing goalie to Matt's Pele.

I dashed into the bathroom and splashed water on my face and arms. It must have been ninety-five degrees in there, but I was shaking as though I'd been shut up in a butcher's meat locker. I couldn't believe what I'd just heard.

Erica was dead! Maybe murdered! God knows, I'd wished her dead, fantasized about it, even plotted it, as, I'm sure, has every other betrayed woman from Medea to Lady Di. But you can't wish someone dead and make it happen. Wishes aren't lethal. How many times have I assuaged some tormented soul's guilt with that little homily.

Okay, so I had some dreams about a dead body. I've had lots of crazy dreams since Rich left. I'm a visual person. I'm instinctive. I've never claimed to be prescient.

When the doorbell rang, my hands were still ice cold, but I was breathing normally. I pressed the buzzer underneath my desk, expecting to see Ruth-Ann's moon face peer around the door.

But it wasn't Ruth-Ann.

It was a uniformed cop and the plainclothes detective who'd let me off the hook yesterday. I wondered later why it registered that his clothes hung loosely on him, as though his appearance were the last thing on his mind.

He looked down at me, flashed his badge. "Lieutenant Brodsky, Bergen County prosecutor's office, Mrs. Burnham." His eyes wandered to the diplomas and certificates on my wall. "Or is it Dr. Carlin?"

"Ms. Carlin," I stammered. "I'm not a doctor. Carlin's my maiden name. I use it professionally." Flustered, I babbled on. "You can't be here about ... your stopping me yesterday. I mean, you said—did you say you're from the prosecutor's office?"

"Crime scene unit. I'm not here about your speeding." He glanced curiously at my double computer setup, with the large TV screen in front of the recliner.

Deliberately I looked at my watch. "I have a patient. She's already late."

"This shouldn't take long."

The uniform took up a position by the door. Brodsky lowered himself into the chair opposite me. Even sitting, his height intimidated me. "What were you doing in Alpine yesterday afternoon?"

"I live in New Jersey."

"You live in Norwood. I stopped you in Alpine."

I was about to lie and say I was visiting an old friend, but just in time, I remembered Sue Tomkins.

"I—I was—I had stopped by—where I used to live."

"You went to your old house?"

". . . Yes."

"Why?"

"Why?"

Because it's home. Because another woman is . . . was living my life.

"Why'd you go there?"

I had a flash of brilliance. "My son wanted to use the pool. I wanted to see if my . . . husband had filled it yet."

"I see." He pulled a small notebook from his pocket and made a note. "Had he?"

"No."

"Couldn't you have telephoned?"

"He . . . was out of town and I don't . . . communicate with his . . . girlfriend."

Why was he asking me these questions? He couldn't possibly believe I'd had anything to do with what had happened to Erica. Should I tell him I knew about her death? He said he was from the crime scene unit. Did that mean the police believed she'd been murdered? Murders are rare in towns like Alpine. He must be aware it was all over the news. I became conscious of the music still playing in the background and decided I'd better come clean. "I . . . heard about—about the accident just now on the radio."

He gave no indication that he'd heard me. "How long have you and your husband been separated?"

"Seventeen months."

Almost to the day. Rich left on Christmas Eve.

"Isn't it usual for the wife to get the house when there are children?"

Damned right.

"Our house is very large, two acres—expensive to maintain. I couldn't possibly . . . I bought a place in Norwood. It's big enough for the children and me, and close enough to Alpine for them to stay in touch with their father. Only problem is, they had to switch schools, so they don't get to see their friends as much as—" I stopped, aware my nervousness was causing me to ramble on.

"Was Erica Vogel named in your action?"

"We've just finished working out the settlement. It could be a few months till we get a court date, and—"

"Would she have been named?"

I couldn't help it. "As what? Whore of the year?"

His mouth twitched. "As co-respondent."

I grimaced. "We're going with no-fault."

"What exactly was Ms. Vogel's position with your

husband's company?" He flipped back through his notes. "I'm sorry, what's it called?"

"Your Face Is My Fortune. Erica started out as a model. Last year she became head of the marketing division." By way of Rich's bed, I wanted to add but didn't.

"And they manufacture . . . ?"

"They manufacture and market products for the skin and hair."

"Mr. Burnham's the president?"

"President, CEO, and chairman of the board."

Rich has a thing about titles.

Brodsky looked directly into my eyes. "Was Erica Vogel the reason your husband left you?"

My mouth went dry. I tried to work up some saliva. "Why are you asking me that? You—you don't think I had anything to do with—with what happened to her?"

"A neighbor saw you late yesterday afternoon at your husband's home. She said you seemed"—he glanced down at his notebook—"'extremely agitated.' When I stopped you for speeding, you were still pretty upset."

"I was upset because she's—she was living in my home, sunning herself by my pool—in my lounge chair. She was on the phone with my husband, planning their wedding! You bet I was upset. But she was alive when I left."

"Did the two of you have words?"

"I don't speak to her. She never even saw me."

"You were close enough to hear her talking on the phone, though."

It wasn't a question.

"Yes, I . . ."

"Was she wearing a bathing suit?"

"My God, was she raped?" Too late, I realized how stupid that sounded. He wouldn't be questioning me if that were the case.

He answered anyway. "It doesn't appear so. She was still wearing the bottom part of the suit."

"That's all she had on when I was there."

He scribbled something in his notebook. "Did you notice if she was wearing any jewelry?"

I could feel the blood rushing to my face. "She . . . had on a gold chain."

Did he know about Rich giving her my necklace? Was I incriminating myself? Should I stop answering questions? *"You have the right to remain silent"* flashed through my mind, legal jargon gleaned from a thousand TV shows. "Is that—is that relevant?"

"Looks like it was torn from her neck in a struggle. Left burn marks."

I grasped at the straw. "Then it was robbery."

"Possibly," he replied, and I knew he didn't think so.

"Was anything else taken?"

"Nothing from the house."

"How do you know?" I persisted. "Maybe some of her other jewelry . . . ?"

"Mr. Burnham indicated everything was there."

A burning sensation began in my stomach. "You didn't tell me how—what happened to her?"

"She was struck over the head and pushed into the pool." He spoke as though he were describing a minor traffic accident. "The blow didn't kill her. She drowned in two feet of water."

I stifled a gasp as my dream came back to me. "Look," I managed, trying not to appear guilty, sure that I did. "I didn't like Erica."

He raised his eyebrows.

"All right! I hated her! You don't love the woman who stole your husband. But that doesn't mean you go out and kill her."

"It does go to motive."

"But I'm not a murderer! I'm a mental health professional, for heaven's sake!"

"I'm not accusing you. These are just routine questions."

Routine?

"A lot of people didn't like her . . . ," I rattled on, unable to follow the advice of all those TV cops.

"Like who?"

My mind went blank. "She—she was a hard woman to work for—to do business with, if she thought she had an edge. She made enemies."

"Could you be a little more specific?"

I didn't want to blurt out names, get innocent people in trouble. "I'd have to think about it."

He pocketed his notebook and rose to his feet. "Well, if you come up with something more concrete, give me a call." He dropped a card on my desk. "And you might think about talking to an attorney."

I stared at him, openmouthed.

"Ms. Carlin," he said, almost indulgently, "you admit to hating Erica Vogel. You were seen at her home around the time of the murder." He held up his hand, cutting off my protest. "You might feel more comfortable getting legal advice. For your own peace of mind." At the door he paused. "Oh, by the way, don't bother sending anyone for your car. We've towed it to the station. Sorry, but we'll need to keep it for a few days." And he shot me a look that froze my blood.

When the blood defrosted enough to meander on up to my brain, it hit me—why the police impounded my car. They were looking for evidence! Maybe for blood traces. For the murder weapon! The old saying popped into my head about being careful what you wish for—you just might get it. Clearly some mischievous deity had granted my wish and was sitting up there having Himself a belly laugh. Because I was the police department's prime suspect!

RUTH-ANN WAS sitting in the waiting room when the door to my office opened and the two cops filed out. She got up so quickly, her chair fell over backward. As he passed by her, Brodsky reached over and set it on its legs. She recoiled as though he were covered with porcupine quills.

Ruth-Ann's parents are Holocaust survivors. They've never gotten over their terror of the police. It's a fear they've unwittingly passed on to their daughter.

"What's happening? What are *they* doing here?" she whispered, after the door had closed behind them.

I masked my own panic with a forced smile. "Oh, it's nothing . . . just—they were asking me some questions about—someone I used to know."

"Are you in trouble?"

"Oh, no, no," I mumbled, brushing past her and sticking a note on the door, telling Vickie I'd had an emergency and would call to reschedule. "But I'm afraid I'll have to cancel today, Ruth-Ann. I'm really sorry, but there's something I have to do." I was having a tough time standing still, and I was edging away when she caught my arm.

"But are they going to let you . . . are you going to be able to have Group tomorrow? Or just on Thursday?"

I couldn't keep the irritation out of my voice. "Of course."

Her lower lip quivered. "I was afraid you—I couldn't stand it if anything—"

"Everything's fine, really. Just—something's come up I have to take care of." Gently I detached her hand. "Call me tonight, and we'll make an appointment for one evening during the week. I promise, okay?"

She backed away, nodding, and I was out of there, running down the street, before she could say another word.

I knew I hadn't handled things well. Ruth-Ann's very fragile right now. A few weeks ago she had a mind-blowing breakthrough, a reliving of a traumatic past experience, and she's still pretty shaky. I'd have to make it up to her at her next session. When I glanced back, she was standing in front of my office building, her arms wrapped around her rotund little body, shivering like one of those orphaned seal pups you see on the Discovery Channel.

"WELL, HAIL, HAIL, the wicked witch is dead. Break out the champagne."

Displaying gleaming white teeth, Meg grinned at me from behind the pristine counter of her café–art shop. Meg's Place is suburban New York's answer to Cheers, only for the foodaholic set. Like my office it's located in the small town of Piermont. Situated on the banks of the Hudson, Piermont is a picturesque community struggling to balance old-world atmosphere with modern commercialism and doing a decent job of retaining its charm. The narrow main street winds through the center of a town that on weekends is congested with tourists bent on finding the ideal gift for the person who has everything, or the perfect antique for that glaringly bare spot in the living room. If the feet give out, there are multiple places to find sustenance, including those gourmet's delights, Freelance Café and Xaviers, run by the talented Kelly brothers. And now, of course, there's Meg's Place.

Meg has decorated her café in shades of green and peach, designed to make you think it's spring all year round. Everywhere you look, you see huge arrangements of fresh flowers, tulips mixed with roses and lilacs and tiger lilies and daisies, surrounded by baby's breath and lush ferns. In the fall and winter, you'd think Meg would go with mums, but she pays the price and makes you believe it's still spring. A great place to be when you're feeling down.

Surrounding the small tables, where customers pig out on gourmet coffee and delectable homemade baked goodies, are shelves displaying sculptures and art objects that Meg takes on consignment and sells. On the wall over the counter, she's hung photographs she herself has taken, photography being her hobby and first love. She once had a show in New York City. For a reason I haven't been able to get her to talk about, she gave up photography as a profession, moved to Piermont, and opened up the café. In less than a year and a half, she's built up a steady clientele.

"You don't understand, Meg. They think I did it!"

"Oh, please. You couldn't kill those carpenter ants that were eating your house."

"Tell that to the police. That detective said I should call a lawyer." I still owed money to Arthur Carboni, my divorce lawyer. The thought of having to hire another lawyer, a criminal lawyer, for God's sake, nearly put me over the edge. "Where am I going to get money for a lawyer?"

"He's just trying to scare you."

"Well, he did. He scared the shit out of me."

Solicitously she placed a cup of chamomile tea in front of me. "Drink. It'll soothe your nerves."

The first time Meg had served me chamomile tea, she'd just moved to town and was preparing for the grand opening of her shop. It was only a few weeks after Rich's precipitous departure.

As I'd stood, stunned, watching him pack, Rich had announced he was going to move in with Erica for a while. "For a while," as though he planned to give me another chance if she didn't live up to expectations. He still loved me, he'd added kindly, but it was a "different" kind of love than he felt for Erica. He might even come back, but right now he needed time off. Time off? From what? Me? Marriage? Car pools?

Just like that. Eighteen years. A marriage. Over. Not even a formal ritual, like walking around me seven times or tossing me back over the threshold.

Weeks later I was still beating myself up, trying to figure out where I'd failed him. Whatever the reason, it no longer mattered. He was gone. Out of my life, and I couldn't accept the awful reality of it. I knew I was making myself sick. I was down to ninety-nine pounds, my hair was falling out, and I'd begun having heart palpitations. I was living proof of the message I used to give my clients at the biofeedback center—your body believes everything you tell it. I was telling it my life wasn't worth living.

That was my frame of mind when I happened to drive by Meg's window display. I was passing through Piermont on my way to Nyack to check out office space when I began to feel dizzy and pulled over by Meg's Place. There was a hole in my stomach the size of Alaska, and I decided to force myself to eat. I wandered into the shop.

Meg was up on a ladder hanging a sepia blowup of an elegant sloop that looked like something out of another, more romantic century. Her long red-gold hair was caught up in a ponytail, and the extra large "Save our Rainforests" T-shirt worn over baggy blue jeans couldn't hide the fact that her figure was spectacular. When she pivoted on the ladder to say "Sorry, I'm not open yet," I wasn't prepared for the face that peered down at me.

Meg has the square chin of a photogenic model and skin so luminous it glows, but her most striking feature is her eyes. They're large and almond shaped, almost oriental, but of a deep aqua-blue. I don't believe I'd ever seen anyone offscreen so stunning. I'm not terrible looking myself—at least, I wasn't before I'd elected to go with the concentration camp look—but next to Meg I felt like the ugly duckling's twin sister. Not exactly what I needed on that particular day.

I mumbled an apology, started backing out, and tripped over a wire. My head met the corner of a cabinet. The searing pain opened the floodgates. The next thing I knew, Meg was leaning over me, handing me a mug and murmuring, "Here, drink this. It'll soothe your nerves."

We've been fast friends ever since.

"You're always in your office till five on Saturdays," Meg was saying. "I can testify to that."

I picked up the delicate porcelain mug and burned my throat downing the boiling liquid, on the off chance she might be right about the tranquilizing effects of herbal teas. "Not yesterday. My patient canceled. I was finished by three."

"Where'd you go after that?" She handed me one of her butter-drenched blueberry muffins. "Someone must've seen you."

I pushed the muffin away, nauseated. "I went for a drive."

"Alone?"

"Yeah."

"Where?"

"Home," I mumbled, avoiding her eyes.

"Home. Well, that's not . . . you don't mean, home—Rich's house?"

Miserably, I nodded. "I don't know why I went there. I just freaked out after Allie told me about the wedding. Erica was by the pool jabbering to Rich on the phone about her damned five-thousand-dollar gown, and she sure as hell was alive! I just watched her for a while, and then I—"

"Anyone see you?"

"Sue Tomkins was out walking her dog. She gave that detective a blow-by-blow of how I was sneaking around and acting weird, and then my car died on the next block and they impounded it, and I think they're looking for the murder weapon." I stopped for lack of oxygen.

"Well, they're not going to find it, so you've got nothing to worry about. This detective—what's his name?"

"Brodsky. Lieutenant Brodsky."

"What's he like?"

"Superefficient, tall, thin, didn't crack a smile."

"I mean was he obnoxious? Did you get the feeling he was trying to trap you?"

"I'm not sure. He was . . . polite, you know, but cold. It was obvious he suspects me."

"They want you to think that so if you're protecting anyone, you'll fold. It's a tactic they use."

"What do you know about police tactics? You probably never even had a parking ticket."

She started cleaning the counter. "I read it somewhere."

"Who would I be protecting? Certainly not Rich."

Meg almost dropped the plate she was holding. "Oh, my God! Rich!"

"What?"

"You don't suppose he told them?"

"Told them what? What're you talking about?"

Meg was usually so unshakable, her alarm undid all the calming effects of the tea.

"What you said the day he left."

"What did I say?"

"Don't you remember?"

"I don't remember anything I did that day."

"About Erica," she whispered. "The scene that night."

It started coming back. Had I told Meg that story? I couldn't remember. "How'd you know about that?"

She began busily brushing crumbs off the counter into her hand. "Didn't you tell me?"

"I don't think so."

"Maybe it was Rich, then."

I didn't think Meg knew Rich well enough to have that kind of discussion. "What did he say I said?"

She didn't look at me, and her voice was so low, I could hardly catch the words, but they transported me back to my old bedroom.

Tears were streaming down my face. Carrying his suitcase, Rich was moving determinedly to the door.

"Rich," I begged, my pride in pieces around my feet, "I love you. We'll work this out. Whatever's wrong, we'll fix it. If you'll just tell me what—"

But I was talking to a robot, a puppet. Someone else was pulling the strings. It was as though a magnet were drawing him out of that room, away from me, from the children, from our past and from our future. And inside me a terrible rage started welling up because I knew exactly on which body part the other end of that magnet was located. I heard the garage door go up. I ran to the window and threw it open.

"Give your whore a message for me, you bastard!" I shouted. "Tell her I'll see her dead and buried and roasting in hell before I see her married to my husband!"

I came back to the present and looked at Meg. She was right, of course. If Rich remembered and told that to the police, my goose was well and truly burned to a crisp!

I DIDN'T GO back to the office. I borrowed Meg's car, drove home, lay down on my bed, and listened to a relaxation tape. I stayed there till I heard the front door slam.

Allie and Matt had gone to a friend's house after I had Meg call and tell them I'd be late. I remembered I'd promised a barbecue, but I dreaded going downstairs to tell them what had happened. I didn't have to. They came flying up the stairs and burst into my room. They'd seen it on a newsbreak while they were watching *Star Trek* reruns.

"Did you know, Mom?" Allie regarded me anxiously.

"Yes, honey, I talked to the police."

"Where's Dad? Was he home?" Matt asked. "Is he okay?"

"He wasn't home when it happened. He got home this morning."

"Then he found her—like that!" Allie's face went two shades whiter, and I pulled her to me.

"Was it a burglar?" Matt asked, jumping up and down. "What'd the police say?"

"The police aren't even sure it wasn't an accident," I said, determined to lessen the impact. "She may have tripped and hit her head when she fell." I avoided mentioning the necklace, which would have unleashed a stream of questions I didn't want to answer.

"Daddy must be—" Allie started, then stopped, not sure of my reaction.

Horton, our mongrel elephant-dog, hungry for his dinner, was nuzzling my legs, and I used him as an excuse to change the subject.

"Horty's hungry," I said, thrusting my feet into my slippers. "You feed him, Matt. Allie'll feed the cats while I get dinner going. Listen, the police are very efficient." Recalling Brodsky, I was pretty certain of that anyway. "They've got everything under control. I'm sure it won't take them long to catch whoever did this."

"What if they don't?" Allie wanted to know. "What if it's a serial killer or somebody like that?"

"Yeah, said Matt. "What if he hated his mother and goes around killing women? And girls," he added, leering at his sister.

"It isn't," I said.

"How do you know?"

"I just do. Now let's go barbecue some chicken!" And I marched downstairs to the kitchen, followed, like the Pied Piper by Allie, Matt, Horton, Luciano, Placido, and the smallest of our Siamese trio, José.

Dinner was unusually quiet. We didn't barbecue out. I broiled the chicken and made frozen peas and instant mashed potatoes.

I caught Allie watching me make little molehills out of the mountain of potatoes on my plate.

"What?" I asked.

"Shouldn't we call Dad?" she whispered.

"Oh, sure," I wanted to snap. *"We wouldn't want him to be lonely."*

But of course I didn't. Instead I replied, "Better to call him tomorrow, sweetheart. The police're probably still there."

Matt's face went uncharacteristically serious. "Was Erica all mushed up when they found her, Mom?"

Allie pushed her chair back and ran from the table. I wanted to do the same, but I kept my voice steady.

"I don't think so, honey. The water cushioned her fall."
I didn't think it was necessary to tell him what drowning
victims looked like.

"Who do the cops think did it?"

"Your mother," I would've said if I were a purist about the
truth.

A lump of mashed potatoes or pure terror choked off
my reply. Thank God, the phone rang. Allie grabbed it in
the living room.

"Mom," she called. "It's Mr. Carboni."

I raced to the living room, determined to keep the conversation short. Calculated at a quarter of his hourly fee,
no call from A. Carboni, Esq., ever cost less than seventy-
five dollars. "Arthur?"

"Carrie, you okay?"

I cleared my throat. "I'm having a kind of crisis."

"I know. I heard." He proceeded to tell me he'd seen it
on a newscast and had called to warn me. "You may start
getting calls from the press."

"Oh, God, I never thought about that."

"Just say you don't know any more than they do and
you have no comment."

I wanted to tell him about Brodsky and ask his advice,
but I didn't want Matt and Allie to hear. "I may need to
meet with you."

"I'm going to be away for a couple of weeks. I assume
this'll put the divorce action on hold for a while."

"I guess so."

"Remember. Don't talk to the media. It could hurt your
case."

"That's what I want to see you about."

"I'll call you when I get back. If you need anything before then, give Rolly a buzz."

His associate. Roland Archer Tobias. Maybe I'm over-sensitive, but would you trust a lawyer whose initials spell RAT?

"Yeah, okay, I will," I fibbed. "Have a nice trip."

It was undoubtedly going to be a very nice trip. I should know. I'd paid for it.

I'd barely hung up when the phone rang again. I grabbed it.

It was Meg. "Carrie, I've gotta split just for a day. I know it's a godawful time to leave you. I'm really sorry. You going to be all right?"

My heart sank. If ever I needed my support system, I needed it now. Besides which there's a part of Meg that's amazingly street-smart, and I value her advice. I wanted to plead with her to wait a few days, but I knew I couldn't.

"Sure. Don't worry."

I knew better than to ask where she was going. Every week Meg disappears for a day or two. She has an arrangement with Franny, the antique dealer from down the street. Franny's a kind of antique herself, who dresses in early-1900s-type clothes that she buys at flea markets and restyles. She only opens her own shop on weekends when the tourists are plentiful and is always happy to pick up a little extra cash baby-sitting Meg's Place.

At first I thought Meg's weekly jaunts had something to do with her passion for photography, because she always took her camera. But I never saw any pictures, and she was invariably depressed when she returned. So naturally I concluded a man was involved.

"I'll try to get back by tomorrow night. And I'll be taking the bus, so you can use my car while the Gestapo has yours."

"Okay. Thanks."

"Don't let that cop character bully you, hear?"

"I'll try not to. Have a good trip, Meg."

Feeling frightened and alone, I hung up. I thought about calling my dad in Massachusetts. We're unusually close. My mother died when I was three and I have no siblings, so the bond between my father and me is a strong one. But he remarried a few years ago and is presently recuperating from a bypass, so I deep-sixed the idea. It would hardly facilitate his recovery to hear that his daughter is a murder suspect.

As I stacked the dishes in the sink, I couldn't stop the wheels turning. If Meg had a lover—a married man, perhaps—knowing my feelings on the subject, I'd be the last person she'd tell. On the other hand, seeing your lover for only a day or two every week seems an awfully unsatisfactory arrangement. Still, in the years I've been practicing, I've come across all kinds of oddball setups. Some high-powered career women deliberately choose married men because it meshes with their lifestyles. Problems with this type only arise if either party suddenly decides they want the whole package—e.g., Erica. The other type are usually women with no self-confidence who are willing to take whatever crumbs their lovers toss their way. Meg doesn't fit either category.

Past conversations with Meg played through my mind. She'd been careful, I realized, never to let anything slip. I had no clue as to where and how she was spending those days and nights.

I was reminded of what she'd said in her shop this afternoon. When had Rich told her about the night he'd left?

Meg knows Rich, of course. She's been at the house several times when he's come to pick up the kids. Maybe the subject had come up when they were making small talk waiting for me to get the children ready.

I dropped the chicken bones into the garbage and started the dishwasher. Then, steeling myself for what was sure to be a difficult conversation, I dialed Rich's number. I wanted him to assure Allie and Matt that he was okay. I planned to pump him about who besides me might have wanted Erica Vogel off the face of the earth, and last, I needed to have the nagging voice in my head silenced. As absolutely disloyal as it made me feel, I wanted to know when he'd had that conversation with Meg.

I let the phone ring a dozen times before I gave up, deciding to catch him at the office in the morning.

The strain of the day was finally sending a painful message to my body. Bone tired, I staggered up the stairs to my room.

Allie's door opened as I got to the top of the landing. "Mom?"

I paused in the doorway. "What, honey?"

"Do you think . . . don't get mad, but d'you think now that—now that Erica is—that maybe—Daddy might come back home?"

The hopeful look on her face turned my insides to mush. I wasn't past longing for a miracle myself.

"I don't think so, sweetheart."

"But he was just—like, you know, infatuated with her. He still loves you. I know he does."

"Allie, a lot has—"

She wouldn't let me finish. "You weren't having fights or anything like Lori's parents. You were happy. Don't you remember?"

I did. My children hadn't been raised in a loveless home, at least not in their formative years, but it made it doubly hard to explain what had gone wrong.

I said what the books tell you to say. "Daddy still loves you and Matt, sweetheart. Very much. That'll never change."

"But if he could change about you—"

"It's different between a man and a woman."

"Well, if that's the way men are, I never want to get married."

I put my arms around my daughter. "Lots of marriages are really good, Allie. And when it works, it's wonderful, because loving somebody, really loving somebody and having them love you back, well, it's just the greatest. And you're going to know that in your life. I know you will, because you deserve it."

"So do you."

"I had it for a while, sweetheart, and maybe I will again. Dad just . . . some men go through a kind of change of life. Like women, only it isn't so much physical.

And they get afraid because they're not young anymore. So they do silly things to try to hang on to their youth."

"But you and Daddy aren't old."

"Right now I feel ninety."

She grinned. "You only look seventy."

"Thank you very much."

"When I finish my homework, can I come sleep with you?"

"Sure." I kissed her shiny black hair, the only part of her like her father. "Make it fast, though. I'll probably be out cold by the time you're done. I'm dead on my feet."

Instantly I regretted the choice of words, but Allie didn't seem to notice. I wondered, as I shed my clothes, if I believed any of the psychobabble I'd just spouted. But Allie was only twelve. Let her have her dreams.

Horton had settled himself on my side of the bed and was alternately twitching and growling, probably pursuing Norwood's entire squirrel population in his dreams. I shoved him over in an effort to make room for Allie. He shifted slightly and quieted down, his snout and one gray and white paw hanging precariously over the edge. Not having the heart to push him the rest of the way, I crawled into my quarter of the bed and spooned myself around his ample rump. The last thought that passed through my conscious mind as I dozed off was, *Could Allie be right?* Now that Erica was out of the picture, could this mutilated marriage possibly be saved?

MONDAY
MAY 24

THE KIDS WERE SUBDUED at breakfast, wondering, I supposed, how they were going to field the questions about Erica at school. Matt would probably relish the limelight. At least at first. Allie would have a hard time of it.

"Who has car pool today?" I inquired brightly.

"Mrs. Rubin," Allie mumbled.

"Better hurry, then. She's always early."

Matt gulped the last of his juice, planted a wet kiss on my cheek, and took off out the door.

Unenthusiastically Allie retrieved her bookbag and followed. " 'Bye, Mom."

I caught her hand. "Allie, it's going to be okay."

She avoided my eyes. I followed her to the door and stood waving until Ellen Rubin's car pulled away. Then I showered and dressed, selecting a plain cotton suit with a skirt to the knee, and a tailored blouse. I was dressing for a part in a play, "working mother, extremely solid citizen." No way could this woman be a murderess, right?

I was thinking clearly this morning and was mad at myself for the half-wish I'd allowed myself last night. It made me painfully aware that I was still not free of Rich.

As I downed the coffee, I planned my day. After seeing my morning clients, I was going to Rich's office. Pumping him for information wasn't going to be easy. Most of the time we kept our conversations to subjects concerning Matt or Allie, but even those had deteriorated of late. The support checks came on schedule; he was good about that. I had not, like some women I know, had to deal with missed payments. He took the kids on his designated weekends, went with them to museums and movies and even an occasional show, but it seemed more duty than desire to spend time with them. They felt it and were confused. It was as though unconsciously he'd gone back to being a bachelor. The father role held no attraction for him anymore. Seventeen years Erica's senior, maybe he thought it made him look old in her eyes.

This morning I was going to be all tea and sympathy, because it seemed to me that Rich or one of his friends or business buddies would have been a witness to Erica's demolishing someone's life or career. People like Erica, who adhere to that "end justifies the means" philosophy, make enemies. Who were her friends? Their friends? Rich's stockbroker and his wife were frequent dinner companions. I made a note to call Gary on the pretext of switching my IRA to a growth fund. There were the guys Rich played racquetball with on Tuesdays. I didn't know if the wives were friendly with Erica or not. I realized I didn't know anything at all about their social life. I didn't know if Rich had kept any of our old friends, because I rarely saw them. I now lived in a different town, and as a single woman, I moved in different circles.

Then I remembered Herb Golinko.

Herb was one of the company admen, a scrawny little chain-smoking guy with only one eye and a twisted mouth made lopsided from nerve damage he'd sustained in the Korean war. He wore an eye patch but, unfortunately, without the Moshe Dayan dash. He was talented, though, and a hard worker. He'd been in the marketing division since the inception of Your Face Is My Fortune, fifteen years earlier. I liked him, and I'd never heard Rich say a bad word about him.

Until Erica.

Erica had humiliated Herb in front of the entire staff. It had happened at a marketing meeting. The story I heard later was that she was in a foul mood that day. Nothing anybody had presented was satisfactory, but when she got to Herb, she was in rare form. It was a crucifixion.

"Jesus Christ, Golinko, that ad's so fucking cockeyed, I should know it's yours! It might look fine to a Cyclops like you, but let me remind you, most of our customers have *two* eyes!" And then she'd proceeded to inform him that she didn't want to see any of his copy till he'd run it by some college kid she'd just hired.

Herb quit the following week. I never heard what happened to him. Maybe he hadn't been able to get another job. Maybe he was homeless, living out of garbage pails on the unfriendly streets of New York City. Maybe he had hated Erica even more than I had!

The motive for the murder hadn't been robbery; apparently nothing except the necklace had been taken. Erica hadn't been molested, so a sex crime was out. A crime of revenge or rage was the only explanation that made sense to me. And to the cops, I was sure. At the moment there was no question in my mind that I remained numero uno on their list of candidates.

As I OPENED the door to the lobby of my office building, my path was blocked by a short wiry guy with a jutting Adam's apple and stringy unwashed hair that hung down to his shoulders. He was wearing dirty sneakers, a washed-out rumpled plaid shirt, and faded skintight jeans. He identified himself as a reporter from the *Phoenix*, a tabloid I recognized from the supermarket. I wondered if it was a condition of employment that its reporters look as sleazy as the content of the paper they worked for.

He planted himself in front of me. "Mrs. Burnham, is it true that Erica Vogel broke up your marriage?"

When I tried to push past him, he grabbed my arm, leaving red marks on my skin. His nose pressed into my face. "Was she sleeping with your husband while he was living with you? Did he leave you for her? How long had the affair been going on till you found out?"

His breath was as offensive as his words.

"Leave me alone!" I jerked my arm free. "I don't have anything to say."

"Wouldn't you like your story told?" he persisted. "You're the wronged woman. Talk to me. I'll tell your side."

"Let me pass. I have to get to my office."

He cornered me, pushed up against me. "She stole your man, and you whacked her, right?" His eyes pinned me, paralyzed me. "You were fighting for your family. Who could blame you? What jury would convict?"

Everything blurred. My throat closed up, and all I could manage was a shake of my head. "No comment, no comment," I got out finally. Not original, but it gave me the impetus to shove him out of my way. I ran to the stairwell, pulled open the door, and fled up the three flights of stairs to my office.

My overeaters were standing around my reception area, little clusters of plump grapes, when I arrived, panting like a marathon runner at the finish line. I managed a shaky smile, told them I'd be right with them, and slipped into my office. I saw Ruth-Ann start toward me before I closed the door, but I waved her away.

"I'm calm, I can cope with this, I'm safe now," I said out loud. I dropped into my chair, struggling to put the unpleasant scene in the lobby out of my mind.

There was a timid knock at my door. I knew it was Ruth-Ann, ignored it. It wouldn't do for her to see me looking frazzled. I'd have to lie, tell her I'd been in the bathroom and hadn't heard the knock.

I'm usually very careful not to do anything to damage Ruth-Ann's self-image. Only five foot two, she weighs a hundred and fifty pounds. But two months ago she weighed a hundred and sixty-five.

When she started in the group, she spent weeks sitting by herself, unwilling or unable to participate. That was when I suggested she come for private sessions on Sundays. We started out doing breathing and relaxation exercises. Then I taught her imagery, where she would visualize herself as slim and self-confident. After several sessions I switched her to brain-wave training, which involves my attaching sensors to the head and earlobes, with the client getting auditory and visual feedback from the computer in an effort to balance the brain waves. The client learns to play computer games, not with a joystick but with his or her brain. Addictive personalities like Ruth-Ann generally produce very little of the dreamy theta brain wave, so I put her on an alpha-theta protocol to help her increase production. At her fourth session she had what is known as an abreaction—a reliving of a past, heretofore repressed memory.

She was sitting across from me, keeping the beeps from the software program pretty constant, which meant her brain was accomplishing the task I'd set for it. I was watching the monitor and saw her theta amplitudes on the graph shoot up above her alpha in what's called a crossover, the time when a client can begin to experience spontaneous imagery.

Her muscle tension measurement suddenly went off the screen. Shaking from head to foot, she emitted an almost inhuman wail like an animal caught in a leg trap.

"*Where are you, Ruth-Ann?*" I asked softly.

"*In . . . his car. In his car,*" she sobbed.

"*Whose car?*"

"*Mr. Woolensky . . . Mr. Wool—he's giving me a ride home. But he's turning down the wrong street! He's stopping the car!*"

"*What's happening? What're you experiencing?*"

"*He's—he's touching me! I want him to stop, but he won't. He has my hand . . . he's making me touch his . . . on his . . . oh, God, he's got his knees between my legs! I can't—I can't get him off! Daddy!*" she screamed. "*Daddy, help me!*"

That day in my office, Ruth-Ann relived every horrific moment of the rape. She was sixteen at the time, a rabbi's daughter. She never told her parents what their neighbor had done to her, never—given her fear of authority figures—considered reporting it to the police, and ultimately forced herself to pretend it was all a dream. After a while her conscious mind believed the story.

But she had begun to eat. In one year Ruth-Ann went from a hundred and ten pounds to a hundred and forty. The next year she gained twenty more pounds. Wrapped in layers of fat, she was safe. The heavier she got, the safer she felt. She had stopped dating, refused to apply to college, and after high school had taken a job as a file clerk, where she was safely hidden away in the back recesses of a musty office. Her parents were distraught. When she came to my overeaters group at the age of twenty-three, Ruth-Ann had given up on having a life.

"Ruth-Ann," I'd murmured when her sobs had abated, "if Mr. Woolensky were here now, if you could talk to him, what would you like to say?"

She'd clenched her fists, and her body went rigid. Tears streamed down her face. "I'd tell him . . . I'd tell him I hate him."

"Tell him," I encouraged her. "Go ahead and tell him."

And then she was screaming. "I hate you, Harry Woolensky! I hate you! I hope someday somebody does this to your daughter! Or your sister! Or your wife! I hope you die!"

Venting her grief and anger was the catharsis Ruth-Ann needed. In the weeks that followed, we worked on several guided imagery exercises in which Ruth-Ann visualized Mr. Woolensky leaving her life. Once we put him in a rocket ship and shot him into outer space. Another time he sailed away in a boat, becoming smaller and smaller until he disappeared.

Ruth-Ann went on a diet, kept to it, and within two months had lost nine pounds. She's doing it herself, but on her list I'm right up there with God. Nice, but there's a downside. I'm not comfortable being God, and Ruth-Ann's attachment to me is beginning to make me uneasy.

Another knock. "Ms. Carlin?"

I pulled myself together. "Be right there. I was in the bathroom," I called out.

Ruth-Ann opened the door, closed it softly behind her. "I heard what that reporter said to you," she whispered.

Damn!

"That's what the police were here for yesterday, wasn't it?"

I nodded. What could I say?

Her brow furrowed. "I heard about your husband leaving you."

"It's almost two years now, Ruth-Ann. I'm okay."

"He must be stupid!"

In spite of everything I laughed. "I certainly think so."

"Do they—do the police think you . . . had something to do with it?"

Oh, God. "They have to question anyone who might've had a reason to—dislike her—you know."

"You mean a motive. They think you had a motive. So does that reporter."

I got to my feet, walked to the door. "He's just looking for a juicy story."

"He's a pig!" Her face flushed. She followed me to the door and whispered in my ear. "My cousin's taking karate. I could get him to beat the guy up for you."

I had to smile at the image of Ruth-Ann's yarmulke-clad cousin slaying my dragon. "Thanks for worrying about me, but I think there's been enough violence."

She shook her head. "People like us—we have to fight back. Tell them 'Never again!' Like the Israelis!"

I put my arm around her. "You can't change other

people, Ruth-Ann. Only how you react to them. Come on, the others are waiting." As I opened the door, I asked casually, "Did anyone else hear that?"

"No. I was walking up. Getting exercise. They all take the elevator."

"Don't say anything, okay?"

She pressed my hand. "I'd never do anything to hurt you."

Two HOURS LATER I nearly put a dent in a black Camry that was straddling two spaces as I parked in the lot outside Rich's building. The executive offices overlook the Hudson River. The view from Rich's window of the city skyline could be used for an "I Love New York" ad.

Erica had redecorated his suite of offices in modern antiseptic, using humongous amounts of glass and marble and white paint, with only occasional splashes of color in the geometric paintings on the walls. It has received much oohing and aahing from her yuppie friends, but I miss the warm wood tones of his old office.

Speaking of warmth, I was greeted decidedly without any by Rich's gal Friday-and-every-other-day, Dot Shea. Old Faithful. Several years earlier she'd seen the light and was "born again." In my opinion once was enough, but if you were Dot, I suppose you'd feel you deserved another shot. Since the advent of Erica, she's tucked her tummy, tightened her tits, decellulited her thighs, and bleached her hair; the "born again" conversion clearly more physical than religious.

Dot had detested me on sight. It took me three years to figure out why; once I did, the feeling became mutual. She's been with Rich since he started the business. Probably knew more about it than he did, but in her eyes he was Christ, or at least Jimmy Swaggart, and she made it her mission to protect him from all life's annoyances. Enter "number one fly" in Rich's ointment: me.

"He isn't here," she snapped without glancing up from her computer.

My heart sank. Rich was my only hope. A place to start. I tried to keep my voice casual so Dot wouldn't suspect how desperate I was, wouldn't guess that I had come for anything other than my monthly check. "When will he be back? I need my check."

"He hasn't been in today. He *is* in mourning, you know."

Rich hasn't missed a day of work since I've known him. That includes the day Matt was born and the day his father died.

"Probably left it on his desk," I mumbled as I walked nonchalantly toward his office. I don't know what I thought I'd find there, maybe his appointment book or Erica's employee evaluation sheets—some clue to give me something to go on.

Dot's voice stopped me. "It's not the first. Your check's not due."

I looked at the smirk on her face, and something clicked. Could she possibly imagine she'd have a chance with Rich if Erica were out of the way? Could her jealousy finally have driven her to *murder*?

"Terrible about Erica," I mumbled insincerely, watching her from the corner of my eye.

She hit the print button and turned to me as the printer hummed into action. "I'd say it'll be a boon to business."

Dot's an equal opportunity hater.

"I can't believe you're hanging any flags at half mast either," she added.

"I never wished her dead." That was a lie, and we both knew it. I felt the stirrings of guilt again. "Anyway, wishing is one thing. Acting on it is something quite different."

Dot laughed, a rasping unpleasant sound. "Whatever you say." She swiveled around to her desk, her fingers flying over the keyboard like a tornado over dry land. Dot's a very capable secretary. I was beginning to wonder just what else she was capable of.

My heartbeat began to outpace her machine as I considered that I might be chatting with a killer. I looked for a place to sit before my knees gave out, perched on the edge of a chair that reminded me of a banana with a shovel on top. "Weekend sure was a scorcher, wasn't it? You managed to get out of town?"

Dot didn't break her rhythm. "No."

"Had to work, huh?"

"I'll tell Richard you were looking for him when he calls in."

I made believe I hadn't heard the implied dismissal. "Yeah, thanks."

"Anything else you want?"

I tried to lean back on the shovel chair and almost fell off. I could see Dot enjoying my discomfort and had an almost irresistible urge to grab that keyboard and smack her over her head. "Come to think of it, there is. Where were you Saturday afternoon?"

"At my sister's the entire weekend. I have an air-tight alibi. How about you?"

I never said Dot was a dope. Maybe she'd persuaded her sister to cover for her so she could hang this murder on me. Killing the proverbial two birds with one stone.

My brow misted with real perspiration. "I don't need an alibi. Rich is out of my life. Erica wasn't worth killing."

"Spoken like a true woman scorned." Her fingers resumed their fandango. "You know, one of the perks for me from your impending divorce is that I don't have to be polite to you anymore. So why don't you fuck off?!"

Religious conversion notwithstanding, I also never said she was a lady. Suddenly I didn't see any percentage in my remaining one. All the repugnance I'd felt watching her fawn over Rich, having to pretend I didn't notice her "office wife" act, exploded like a geyser erupting. I flew across the room, leaned across her desk, my face two inches from hers. "You sick, deluded fool!" I hissed. "What the hell do you think you're playing at?"

Taken aback by my ferocity, she recoiled. "Get away from me, or I'll call Security."

"Go ahead! See if Gus'll throw me out!"

She started to get up, but I trapped her between her chair and the computer table. "You think I haven't noticed your cutesy little wifey-game all these years, haven't guessed you saw yourself honeymooning in Europe, dining at Le Cirque, hostessing all those lavish little soirées for the company clients?"

"You're crazy!"

"Not crazy. Mad. But I'm going to do you a favor and give you some good advice. Get a life, because it's never gonna happen. Rich uses you like he uses everyone, and he'll dump you like he did me when he doesn't need you anymore. So I wouldn't put a deposit on that wedding dress just yet."

Her face went ashen. I'd shocked her speechless. I actually felt a little ashamed but decided to take advantage of her temporary paralysis. I strode determinedly toward Rich's door.

"I'm going to make a call from this office. See that I'm not disturbed."

I slammed the door behind me and locked it. There was dead silence in the other room. Either I'd caused a heart attack, or she'd gone for Gus. My money was on the latter, so my search time would be limited.

What first caught my eye nearly sent me into cardiac arrest. On the wall opposite Rich's massive oak and ebony desk was a life-size photograph of Erica. I recognized it as a blowup of a lipstick ad she'd done when she worked for him as a model before she was promoted to marketing director. She was wearing a pink-flowered low-cut dress, her assets displayed as though she were selling her wares instead of the company's. I had the chilling feeling those calculating ice-blue eyes were following me as I moved around the room.

I forced myself to focus on Rich's desk. Not one

picture, not even of his children. It was clean except for a Lucite desk set. A Lucite desk set. What had become of the leather set Dot had given him for his birthday? I could imagine her reaction when she'd realized her gift had become a casualty of Erica-mania. Brushing past a white damask silk sleep sofa—as out of place in an office as a polar bear in the tropics—I hurried to the desk and riffled through the top drawer. Company stationery, envelopes, all what you'd expect. Quickly I searched the other drawers. Nothing helpful. I wondered if there was a safe. Where would Rich keep the company books? What should I look for if I found them?

About to close the bottom drawer, I noticed a jumble of keys crammed together at the rear. Scooping them up, I laid them out on the desk. Two I recognized as belonging to the Alpine house; most could have been to anything. But one was attached to a sterling silver key ring shaped like a heart and with the initials D.S. clearly engraved in the center.

Why would Rich have the keys to Dot's apartment? Surely he wasn't involved in an intimate way with *her*? Not Rich, who hired and fired gorgeous models every day of the week. There could be a thousand reasons why Rich would have Dot's keys. Like . . . this was where she parked an extra set in case of emergency. Or maybe he'd stopped by to feed her cat when she went on vacation. Except I was pretty sure Dot didn't have a cat. I was nine hundred and ninety-nine reasons short, still working on it, when I heard the lock turning. I just had time to return all the keys but Dot's, which I dropped into my jacket pocket. The door swung open. I looked up into the dark-ringed, angry eyes of the stranger who used to be my beloved.

"**W**HAT'RE YOU DOING here?"

Every time I see Rich, I have to make a conscious effort to remember we're no longer connected.

He looked drained. I could tell he'd been drinking. His complexion was blotched and ruddy, and a toddler would have been steadier on his feet.

Rich is a big man, even-featured, broad-shouldered, with the beginnings of a middle-age paunch that he takes great pains to camouflage behind well-tailored clothing. Only those of us privileged to have viewed him in the buff (which, I was coming to suspect, may have included a large percentage of the tristate area's female population) would be aware of it. It was a shock to see him unshaven, his usually well-styled thick black hair unkempt, his shirt tail crumpled and hanging out of pants that looked like a dog had mistaken them for a chew toy. Chances were he'd been wearing those clothes since Sunday morning. I hoped that was it, because even sober, Rich would be furious at finding me going through his things. Smashed, he might be—really unpleasant.

I sidled around the desk, relieved he didn't seem to notice that I'd taken over his chair. Some perverse piece of me, responding like Pavlov's dog to old conditioning, wanted to reach out and comfort him. Another piece ached to crawl into his arms and have my own fears lulled.

Old habits die hard.

"The kids," I began. "They're scared, Rich. They need you. All this media attention has really—"

"Come to gloat, have you?"

I drew back. "That's a horrible thing to say!"

He pushed past me and flopped onto the sofa. "Come on, you hated her. You wanted her dead."

"Apparently I wasn't the only one," I protested, flushing. "Maybe you ought to be thinking about who else had reason to feel that way instead of attacking me."

He buried his face in his hands, and his tone suddenly altered. "It's been awful, Carrie. You can't imagine. Finding her like that . . ." A shudder traveled through him, and he lifted his head and looked at me in a way that, in the old days, would have had me rubbing his back and serving up enormous portions of wifely sympathy. Oddly, I was moved even now. Seeing him hurting, vulnerable, brought memories of closer times flooding back.

"I know," I murmured, patting his shoulder. "You must be—"

"Don't know how I'm going to manage without her."

My hand stopped midpat as my sympathy evaporated like summer mist. I remembered his protestations of undying love to me. "You're a survivor. You'll survive."

He shook his head. "She was a marvel. Tough, mean when she had to be. A take-charge person. Sales went through the ceiling after she took over."

And it hit me! Rich hadn't left me for another woman, per se. He'd left me for a take-charge *business* woman who could send sales through the ceiling! Granted, one with undeniable physical attributes, but the bottom line was the bottom line with Rich, even where Erica was concerned.

"Bastard cops were grilling me this morning. Me, the bereaved, while I was trying to make funeral arrangements!"

"Maybe they think you can help—"

"No, no, I'm a suspect, can you believe it? Assholes kept on about her having other men." He grabbed my arm. "I s'pose they got that from you?"

I jerked away. "I'm afraid I wasn't privy to Erica's affairs."

"She'd never've cheated on me!"

God, the ego!

He lurched to his feet. "I need a drink."

I remembered the kids telling me he had a fully stocked paneled bar concealed someplace behind these sanitary walls. You pressed a button, and shazam! like magic, a wall opened. I slid off the desk, blocking his path. "Don't. You've got to keep a clear head."

He pushed me out of the way and staggered toward the bathroom. "Gotta pee."

I waited till I heard him splashing water on his face. "You sure there wasn't anybody else?" I called out. "An old boyfriend, maybe? Somebody she jilted for you? Or somebody she annihilated at work, maybe? Like poor Herb Golinko? Whatever happened to him?"

A pause. I heard the water turned off.

"Dunno."

"She ruined his career, and you let her. Hell, we both know she wasn't Mother Teresa. Who had a grudge—?"

"Nobody, goddammit. Except you."

"You think I did it?"

"Well, why . . ." He appeared in the doorway, stopped. "Oh, I get it. You'd be right up there with me on the cops' list of most likely."

"Don't be ridiculous. I wasn't even around over the weekend."

"Where were you?"

I'm a lousy liar. I can never think fast enough. "The kids and I went with Meg for the weekend."

"Meg was working. She didn't leave until last night."

Just for a second the room spun. "How'd you know that?"

"Allie told me. Why'd you lie?"

"When did you talk to Allie?"

"She called me before she left for school. Don't change the subject."

"Have you been seeing Meg?" I held my breath.

He stared at me blankly. If it was an act, it was a good one. "What're you talking about?"

I exhaled . . . decided to believe him. "How about Dot?"

His timing was a little slower on that one.

"She's my secretary, f'chrissake! You think I fuck everything walks into the office?"

I bit off my retort.

He walked over to the desk, started pulling open drawers.

"What're you looking for?"

"Aspirin. Head feels like it's gonna explode."

I pulled a two-pack out of my bag, tossed it at him. "Erica ever get any threatening calls?"

He ripped open the packet and swallowed the pills without water. "Will you give it a rest? I told you—"

"Someone hated her enough to kill her, Rich. You have to know it wasn't me. And you know it wasn't you. So we have two fewer on our list than the police. You're probably the only one knows enough about her to put it together."

"Don't you think I'd've told the police if I had a clue, goddammit?"

I tried shock treatment. "How much do you really know about her past? Those affairs the police were talking about? Everyone in the company knew she slept her way up from the factory foreman to you. Maybe somebody halfway up the ladder—?"

That got him in his fat ego. "Shut up! Just shut up! Christ, the woman's dead! She's dead, and you're still bad-mouthing her!"

I saw red. I *was* a woman scorned, and hell couldn't come close to matching my fury. "You're right!" I shouted. "I should be cursing you!"

"Who the hell are you to play Miss Innocent?" he bellowed. "How can I be sure it wasn't you killed her? You lied about being away. You call her a whore every damned chance you get! You said you'd see her dead and buried before you'd see us married!"

He hadn't forgotten! I lost it completely then. "What'd you expect?" I yelled back. "That I'd throw a party welcoming her into the family?"

He strode to the door. "I'm outta here. I don't need to listen to this crap."

I grabbed his arm. "Oh, yes, you do! For once in your

miserable, self-centered life, you're going to listen! Because this time she damned well pissed off the wrong person. Somebody even tougher and meaner than she was, somebody who wasn't going to take it. And for a change, this time, the sky didn't fall in on foolish little Henny-Penny. This time, it was her and you who paid the price!" I stopped, out of breath. And nerve.

Rich was standing over me, clenching and unclenching his massive fists. I wasn't a hundred percent sure I wasn't about to become a battered wife. I stepped back.

His mouth worked, but nothing came out. Then he managed a croak. "You did it, didn't you?" His face turned purple. "You did it to get back at me! You killed Erica!"

Before I could answer, the door was flung open. Out of my peripheral vision, I caught Dot's triumphant expression. Behind her, staring at me, mouth agape, stood Gus Gennaro, Rich's normally jolly security guard, looking as though someone had just whacked him in the gut with a battering ram.

I don't remember running past Gus or Dot, or pressing the elevator button, or riding the elevator to the lobby. I think I used the stairs, but I wouldn't swear to it in a court of law. Somehow I found myself in the parking lot racing to the safety of Meg's car. I fell to my knees beside the rear tire and lost what was left of my breakfast. Then I burst into tears. I'm not sure if they were the result of the past couple of days, or grief over love gone rancid, but I cried all the way back to the office as though I'd lost my best friend.

Which I certainly had.

THERE WAS A message on my answering machine when I arrived back at the office. Joe Golden, Vickie Thorenson's psychiatrist, wanted me to squeeze her in for a relaxation session. Joe sends me patients on a regular basis. He's one of the few psychiatrists I know who appreciates the benefits of biofeedback, so I always try to accommodate him. After this morning I probably needed a session with him more than Vickie needed one with me, but I'd blown her off yesterday, so I called Jen Cordova's mother and asked if she'd mind picking up her daughter directly from school and bringing her to my office by three-fifteen. Jen's one of my ADD's on her next-to-last session and is now getting B's in school, so I knew I could finish with her in three-quarters of an hour. I called Vickie and arranged to see her at four.

Somehow I managed to put the incident with Rich in a separate compartment of my mind. Necessary, so I could concentrate on what I had to do. Keeping busy, the best therapy. I checked my book, saw that I had Baji Ponamgi at twelve-thirty, Carl Lomax at one-thirty, Phyllis Lutz at two-thirty, and Timmy Brannigan, another ADD, at five.

Mr. Ponamgi's a pain patient, fifties, an uptight accountant, referred to me by my old clinic. Quite a coup, considering they have two biofeedback therapists on staff. He was in an automobile accident last March and has pain in the cervical and lumbar regions, meaning whiplash, and back injury. Difficult areas to treat, especially in an A-personality type like Mr. Ponamgi, who thinks he'll be struck dead by the God of Workaholics if he allows himself a day off. But he's making progress. He works as hard at healing himself as he does at everything else, and being East Indian, he's more open to alternative therapies than many westerners.

Carl's the complete opposite. Only thirty-eight, sinewy, and basically in good shape, he had a minor accident on the job, gets workman's comp, and if he can get away with it, will probably milk the system forever. He stonewalls me at every turn.

Phyllis is my only hypochondriac. She had both hands pressed to her head and was already pacing the waiting room impatiently when I finished with Carl at two-twenty.

"I'm getting a migraine," she announced to Carl.

"That right?" he replied. "I got a spinal injury, I'm in constant agony," winning the "can you top this" contest hands down.

"Come on in, Phyllis," I cut in quickly before she could start enumerating her gastrointestinal symptoms. Phyllis spends half her time in her internist's office and half in mine attempting to treat her headaches and her nervous stomach, which have their origin in the fact that her husband isn't and never will be Donald Trump. I've talked with Greg Lutz. He's a decent guy who makes an adequate living, but if Phyllis can't have the jet-set lifestyle, she'll opt for the attention illness brings her.

"This isn't working," she declared the minute she had settled herself in the recliner.

"It isn't for everyone," I agreed. "But you've only had five sessions and nothing else has helped, so why not stick with it for a while longer?"

She picked a piece of lint off her cashmere skirt. "The whole concept makes no sense. Warming my hands. Ridiculous."

"Have you been practicing?"

"I feel silly."

"No one has to know what you're doing. Let's try it." I flipped on my tape recorder and began attached the sensors to her head and fingers. I felt her body stiffen under my touch. "What's the matter?"

"You always do that?"

"What?"

"Record the sessions? I never noticed."

"It's so I can review what I've done, what works and what doesn't with a particular patient. Does it bother you?"

"Yes. Turn it off. I don't want any record of something I might say when I'm under."

"Under what?"

"Hypnosis."

"Phyllis, I don't hypnotize you. I relax you. It's more self-hypnosis than anything."

"I don't care. Just turn it off."

I complied. "Okay, we'll just have music then."

It was a frustrating session for us both. Sun on the beach didn't work, hot oil didn't work, even boiling lava and volcanic ash failed to de-ice those frigid extremities. The more images I came up with, the lower her peripheral temperature dropped. At the end of the session, my hands were sweating and her temperature read a chilly seventy-nine degrees. She left clutching her temples, heading for Dr. Heller's office. Feeling like a failure, I took two aspirin.

I was actually happy to see Vickie, who was only ten minutes late—a record for her. She appeared more relaxed when she walked through my door than I'd expected after Allie's melodramatic description of their phone conversation. As always, she looked gamine adorable. The doe-shape of her big brown eyes and that heart-shaped face allow her to get away with one of those boyish haircuts you never have to set, and if she were to decide to wear a horse blanket, her long lean dancer figure would make it look like a Donna Karan. Today she wore brown stretch pants, a tie-dyed tunic top, and a carefree smile.

I'm always struck by Vickie's abrupt mood changes. Ever since I've known her, the on-again, off-again nature of the relationship with her lover has kept her seesawing between rapture and despair. Happily, whatever combination of medication and counseling Dr. Golden had come up with today seemed to have had a settling effect.

"I'm sorry about canceling your appointment yesterday," I apologized as I attached the sensors to her fingers and muscles. "I had an emergency and had to leave the office."

"That's okay. Dr. Golden saw me this morning."

"I know. But I felt bad about it because my daughter said you sounded really upset when you called on Saturday."

"I was, but it's over. I guess I'm learning to deal with it."

"With what?"

"That my dad hates me."

"Oh, Vickie, he doesn't hate you. He just wants to control you." My eyes flashed to the computer, and I noted that her EDR, which was registering internal tension, went from seven to thirty-nine as she talked about her father. "What happened this time?"

"Same old stuff." She began twirling the spiral on my desk with her free hand. "He was screaming at me, calling me names. He'd like to keep me locked up in a cage."

Much of the work Joe Golden and I had been doing with Vickie had to do with getting her to deal with her feelings of anger toward her father.

"Did you do what we talked about?"

"You mean about just walking away?"

"And the visualization exercise."

She giggled. "Yeah. You should've seen the expression on his face when I said, 'I'm leaving. I don't allow anyone to abuse me anymore.' And then I walked out of the house and got in my car and went over and over the exercise in my head."

"Good for you." I didn't like Vickie's father. I'd met him a couple of times when he'd brought her to the office before she had her car. He's a domineering man who thinks money can buy him anything, including his daughter's love and respect. I suspected Vickie's promiscuity was related to her endless search for a father substitute. "I was worried you might've been feeling depressed over—you know, the breakup."

"Oh, no. I fixed that too. We're getting back together."

I was tempted to go on about the follies of staying in a bad relationship but caught myself. Instead, once she was completely relaxed and in a meditative state, I gave her positive affirmations about taking charge of her life and making things happen instead of passively letting them happen to her.

I should follow my own advice, I thought wryly. We mental health professionals are so good at teaching other people how to handle their problems, not always roaring successes in dealing with our own.

By the end of the hour, Vickie's muscles registered 0.4 and 0.6 respectively, indicating a completely relaxed physical state, but her excitement at the prospect of being back with her lover was clearly keeping her emotions at a high pitch. I hadn't been at all successful at lowering her EDR or in raising her peripheral temperature to a balanced ninety-two degrees. Then I remembered what it felt like—being young and in love—and despite my certainty that this particular relationship was a dead end for Vickie, I couldn't help feeling just a tiny pang of envy.

THE LAST PERSON in the world I wanted to see was waiting outside my office building when I came out after work.

I'd been looking forward to going directly home and soaking in a bathtub filled with stress-reducing crystals, when I saw Brodsky's lanky frame holding up a telephone pole. Pretending to search through my bag for my keys, wishing he would vanish, I hurried toward the lot, where I'd parked Meg's car. He caught up with me as I got to the gas station on the corner.

"Sorry about this," he murmured, falling into step beside me.

"About what, Lieutenant? I've told you everything I know."

"Just a few more questions. Thought you'd prefer not to come down to the precinct."

I didn't miss the implication. My knees went weak, and I stumbled.

He caught my arm and steadied me. "Let's take a walk."

I shook free, shrugged my assent, not slackening my pace. The heat wave had broken, and the temperature had returned to normal, somewhere in the seventies. I headed for the pier and breathed in the clear, crisp air.

He waited until I stopped at the water's edge. "How long would you estimate you spent watching Ms. Vogel?"

I hesitated. "Maybe—maybe twenty minutes to half an hour."

"Can you pinpoint the exact time?"

"Somewhere between three-thirty and four, I should think. Is that important?"

"Could be. If you can prove it. Depends on when the M.E. fixes the time of death."

"Sue Tomkins saw me."

"She doesn't remember exactly what time she walked the dog. Did anyone else call Ms. Vogel beside your husband while you were there?"

"No."

"Their conversation was friendly?"

I gazed out over the water, focusing on the line of rush-hour cars crawling like an army of ants over the Tappan Zee, willing myself to feel nothing. "Yes."

"Did Ms. Vogel leave her chair at any time? Did she go inside at all?"

"No."

He jotted something down in his notebook. "Could you give me an accurate description of the necklace she was wearing?"

"I thought my husband did that."

"Men tend not to notice detail."

Involuntarily, my hand crept to my throat as if to finger the familiar links. "It was a gold watch fob chain— old, maybe late eighteen hundreds. The links were rect-angular, about half an inch long each, with little pieces of chain holding them together."

His pencil passed midpage. "You seem to have a rare eye for detail, considering you said you never got close to her."

"The necklace had been mine." I kept my face expres-sionless. "Rich will be entitled to half my jewelry when we're divorced. Erica wanted that piece, so he made off with it a little ahead of time."

He began writing again. "I wasn't aware that personal possessions are part of equitable distribution in New Jersey."

"Jewelry is. Most men don't take advantage of it."

I felt his eyes on me. I kept mine on a sea gull that was shoving a smaller gull off its perch on a stanchion. Nature's way. Survival of the toughest.

"Rough seeing something you valued on another woman," he said.

I shifted my gaze and looked him straight in the eye. "Hardly worth killing over."

He looked back down at his notes. "Anything else you can tell me about the necklace?"

"The clasp was an addition. I guess Erica thought the

original was too plain. Or maybe she found it hard to fasten. Whatever, he replaced it with a cluster of diamonds and rubies. It didn't go with the chain."

He studied me for a minute. "How did you happen to know that?"

"What?"

"That the clasp had been replaced."

I grimaced. "She wore it to Allie's Sunday school graduation last week. She made sure I saw it."

"Did you notice anyone in the area when you drove there on Saturday? Anyone who didn't seem to belong in the neighborhood, anything unusual at all?"

I thought hard, trying to dredge up something. "There may've been," I said finally, "but I didn't notice anything."

"You know all the neighbors' cars?"

"Pretty much. It's not a long street."

"Was there an unfamiliar car parked anywhere? Most people park in their own driveways or garages. Was there a car or truck parked on the street?"

I tried to imagine how the street had looked, but all that came back to me was the indelible image of a half-naked Erica wearing my necklace, lounging on my outdoor furniture. I shook my head. "I'm sorry. I can't remember."

"Too bad."

"How about fingerprints?" I asked hopefully. "You must've found fingerprints."

"We did," he replied succinctly. "Yours."

In my youth I used to break out in a rash whenever I got nervous. At Brodsky's words I was sure hives were popping out all over. "*Mine*? Where?"

"There was a clear thumbprint on a plastic boomerang we found near a willow tree."

My fantasy sprang to mind. "What do you think I did? Boomeranged Erica to death with a child's toy?"

"I didn't say it was the murder weapon."

"I picked it up. I told you I'd been in the yard."

"Good you did. Because there was detritus on the floor mats of your car that matched the kind found on the grounds. There was also blood," he said, as an afterthought.

I could barely get the word out. "Blood?"

"Not Ms. Vogel's. You must've cut yourself on the brambles. Probably weren't even aware of it."

I recalled the sharp edge of the boomerang. "How could you know . . . ?" And then I remembered. When I had applied to teach a night course at Tenafly high school several years back, I'd had to get fingerprinted at the police station. Routine for any town employee.

"I hope you're not planning a vacation. It'd be best if you stuck around. And I hope you took my advice and got in touch with a lawyer."

I shook my head, not trusting my voice. How could I explain to this detective that people like me don't know criminal lawyers? We don't even know other people who know criminal lawyers. Do they list them in the yellow pages? I wondered. I could picture the ad: *Blank and blank, experienced trial attorneys—rapists and murderers, our specialty.*

He snapped his notebook closed. "Up to you. Your car will be returned to you this evening. Need a ride home?"

High up on my list, a ride in a police car. "I've borrowed a car. I think I'll stay here for a while."

He didn't leave right away, just stood watching me from under hooded lids.

"I'm not going to jump, if that's what you're afraid of," I muttered, unable to stand the scrutiny.

"Didn't think you were the type. Take it easy now." And he sauntered back the way we had come.

Take it easy?

I sat on the wooden bench the town provides for tourists and tried to remember what our street had looked like that afternoon. I thought about Sue Tomkins. Nothing ever escapes Sue's notice. Except, of course, I thought wryly, what time she'd decided to walk the dog last Saturday. But if there had been a car or van or truck on our street, Sue would surely remember. I knew Brodsky had questioned her, but maybe she'd been too rattled about the murder and hadn't been thinking clearly. Making a mental note to call her, I watched the sea gulls as they floated on the wind, wishing I had their wings, wishing I could absorb by osmosis the peace they exuded.

After a while I walked back to Meg's car and drove home.

MATT WAS SUBDUED when I walked in the door, failing to greet me with his usual hug. I kissed him on the top of the head and headed for the kitchen, calling over my shoulder that we were having pork chops and he should go wash up and set the table. It was important for the kids to believe their lives were going on as usual.

"Mom, bunch of messages on the machine," Allie yelled from upstairs.

"Didja remember applesauce?" Matt shouted from the bathroom.

Well, that was normal.

One of Rich's legacies to our children: Applesauce goes with pork chops, cranberry sauce with chicken, mint jelly with lamb. *Shouldn't take a genius to remember to buy them together, right, sweetheart?*

Luckily, fortune was smiling on me and I found a jar of Mott's Chunky nestled behind a box of Kraft's macaroni and cheese. I put it on the table in the dining area of our combination kitchen–family room. We practically live in this one sunny room. It's become a ritual, me cooking, Allie sprawled out on our deep-cushioned chintz couch, reading, while Matt does his homework at the table. It makes for a kind of togetherness and sharing that had eluded us in our more spacious quarters.

The small dining room serves as a home office for me. No more formal dinner parties entertaining buyers. I don't miss giving the parties, and I don't miss the high-powered money talk. On occasion I admit I do miss my marble-tiled bathroom with the built-in Jacuzzi, but only when it's been one of those days that make you want to crawl back into the womb. Like today.

I pressed the playback button on my answering machine and began cutting up vegetables for a salad.

"Carrie, honey?"

Meg was back.

"You still need my car, or have the storm troopers released yours? Give a call. I'm at your disposal day or night."

Relief flooded through me at the sound of that comforting voice. I was about to call her when the next message played.

"Phyllis Lutz, Ms. Carlin. Just wanted you to know I was up all night with a migraine. I don't think you're helping me. I'm seeing Dr. Heller again today. I'll call you if I decide not to keep my Friday appointment."

I heard the click and waited for the next message. It was Vickie, asking if she could set up another appointment; would I please get back to her. Just before the tape cut off, I was certain I heard her father's voice, certain I heard him shouting "goddamned tramp." I resolved to call Vickie back as soon as I'd spoken to Meg.

The minute I heard Meg's voice, my suspicions about her and Rich vanished. "Meg?"

"Carrie, hi. How're you doing?"

"Meg, I'm going to need a—a criminal lawyer. You know anyone who knows one?"

A pause. "They haven't charged you, have they?"

Was there an unspoken *yet* in that pause?

"No, but Brodsky was asking me more questions. And he keeps advising me to get one. I think I should."

"Lemme make some calls. I'll get back to you."

"Okay." I felt like a child, dumping my mess into a competent adult's hands. "Meg?"

"Yeah?"

"I'm glad you're back." I could feel her warmth through the phone.

"Keep the faith, kid."

TUESDAY
MAY 25

THE NEXT AFTERNOON
Brodsky showed up at my office again. He was standing in
front of my door when I came out of the elevator. I'd just
returned from lunch at Meg's. She'd given me a pep talk
and the names of two lawyers she'd obtained from a
friend, and I was feeling better. Until I saw him. His
shoulders were hunched inside his loose brown jacket,

and there was a fine white line around his mouth that didn't look as though a smile could get past it.

"We seem to have a missing person on our hands," he said, skipping the preliminaries.

"Excuse me?"

He moved aside as I inserted the key into the lock. "Any idea where your husband is?"

"At his house or his office, I presume."

"When'd you last see him?"

Did he know what had transpired between us?

"Yesterday."

Brodsky's face was impassive. I couldn't read his expression.

I cleared my throat. "I thought you're not a missing person unless you've been missing for at least a couple of days."

"Under ordinary circumstances that would be true."

Was I being accused of kidnapping now? "Maybe he had a rendezvous," I muttered with an edge to my voice. "Not even snow, nor sleet, nor the murder of his intended will keep our Richard from his appointed bed."

He was scowling as he held the door open for me. "This isn't a joke."

"I wasn't joking."

He followed me into my office and sat in my client chair. "Mind if I sit?"

I wondered why he bothered to ask. I shrugged. "What makes you think Rich is missing?"

He stretched out his long legs and loosened his tie. "He was supposed to be at the precinct this morning. He never showed. When we checked, it looked as though he hadn't been home. His car's still in the lot."

That *was* strange. I began to feel uneasy.

"No one seems to know where he is."

I stayed on my feet. It was a power thing. "Ask Dot Shea. She makes sure he checks in with her twenty times a day."

"She didn't show up for work today either. And she doesn't answer her phone."

I couldn't see Rich involved with Dot, but I said it anyway. "Well, there's your answer. Check the motels."

"Timing's lousy."

"We're talking about a man who left his family on Christmas Eve. He flunked Timing a year and a half ago."

"Want to tell me about your meeting?"

I hesitated. "I wanted him to talk to the kids. All this is very frightening to them. So I went to the office, and . . ."

"And?" he prompted.

I could tell he knew about the fight. Gus must've given him an earful. "We had . . . a disagreement."

Something faintly related to a smile pushed its way past the white line. "I hear it was the War of the Roses."

"I went there because I thought he might come up with something useful. Things got out of control."

"Playing detective?"

He was amused in that damned superior male way. I wanted to punch him.

"Listen, I'm not stupid. You people think I'm guilty. If I don't find out who killed Erica, you'll probably throw me in jail."

"Every time I come to this office, it's not to arrest you, Mrs. Burn—" He glanced at my nameplate. "Which do you prefer? Burnham or Carlin?"

"Why don't you just call me Carrie?" I said. "It works with both names."

Method to my madness. You can't call anyone you believe to be a murderess by their given name.

He shrugged and said awkwardly, "Well—Carrie, it doesn't look good, your husband disappearing just now."

"Not good for whom?"

"He was advised to stay put. The fact that he took off . . ." He let the sentence hang.

From out of the corner of my eye, I watched him as he absentmindedly spun the spiral I keep on my desk for patients who don't know what to do with their hands. "He's probably not thinking clearly. When I saw him, he was pretty upset."

"Aren't you?"

"I wasn't in love with Erica."

The spiral spun around and around. "Did you know about the row in the minister's study?"

"Rich had a row with the minister?"

"With his intended."

At least all hadn't been peachy-keen in paradise. "Over what?"

"He wanted her to sign a prenuptial."

"No kidding!" So Rich hadn't entirely lost his marbles.

"The minister said they almost came to blows. She nearly called off the wedding."

I was delighted to hear it. But they had apparently

worked things out, because there'd been no mention of agreements, signed or unsigned, in the phone conversation I'd overheard. I said so.

"So you don't think he did it?"

Shocked, I asked, "Do you?"

He shrugged. "I keep my options open."

"Rich isn't a violent man."

"Moment of passion. In a rage."

I shook my head. "He's not a passionate man either."

"Does he drink? Do drugs?"

"Not drugs."

"But he drinks."

"Well, yeah, sometimes."

"Excessively?"

"He's not an alcoholic, if that's what you mean. He never loses control—" Then I stopped, because I recalled a night a month before Rich had moved out.

We'd gone to dinner for our anniversary at the Union Square Café on Sixteenth Street, in the city. It was a place we reserved for special occasions. I gave Rich a sleek Rado watch I'd saved up for months to buy to replace his old Seiko. He got an odd expression on his face and asked if I'd mind if he exchanged it, he didn't need a watch.

"Rich, you've had that Seiko forever. The Rado is so—"

"This isn't my Seiko. It's a Rolex."

Dumbstruck, I stared at his wrist. "A Rolex? Where'd you—"

"A customer I did a favor for."

It must have been quite a favor. I should have left the restaurant then. I should have left him then. But I didn't. I just sat there trying to believe that story, trying not to think about the emerald earrings Erica had been flashing around the office.

He handed me my gift—a pearl pin that looked like old teeth. I gritted my teeth and said it was beautiful. Beyond that we hardly spoke. Rich was drinking heavily. Heavily into denial, I kept a smile on my face, but it felt painted on, as though I were a wooden puppet. I don't remember what I ordered. Whatever it was, I'm sure it was delicious, and I'm equally certain I didn't eat it.

It was snowing and very cold as we walked back to the car. Rich offhandedly dropped the news that he'd be away on business over the Christmas holidays. I stopped walking, my heart gone as cold as the snowflakes on my lashes.

"On Christmas? You have business meetings on Christmas?"

Everything came together then. The Rolex, Rich's frequent "business" weekends, the marked change in the quality of our sex life, Erica's late-night calls needing Rich's advice on some design or other, the time we'd gone to a party and she'd taken his arm—very possessively, I'd thought, for an employee—to introduce him to a buyer. When I'd protested, Rich had put me off, saying Erica was a "touchy-feely" kind of person, that she did that with everyone. So on that snowy night in November, I asked Rich if he was taking touchy-feely Erica with him. When he didn't answer, I knew. I threw myself at him, my fists pounding on his chest while tears of fury and despair gushed from my eyes. The next thing I knew, I was in a snowbank, with my head a quarter of an inch away from a lamppost.

"Remember something?"

My reverie was abruptly terminated by Brodsky's quiet voice. "It's not significant. He didn't mean . . . it was—brought on by unusual circumstances."

"So are most murders. Want to tell me about it?"

Rich had accused me of murder. Why was I so reluctant to implicate him. "No," I said. "I don't."

"Okay." He got to his feet. As he passed the computer desk, he paused, fingering a set of sensors hanging off one of the hooks. "What're these for?"

"They measure EDR—electrodermal response. Level of stress. Kind of like a lie detector."

"Looks like we're kind of in the same business."

"No. What I do *reduces* tension."

This time he did smile. "Think about what I said. You don't owe this man a thing anymore."

I remained silent.

"And for the record," he added, "while I believe you wished Ms. Vogel drawn and quartered, I don't think you did anything about it."

My own EDR went through the roof. "Why all of a sudden?"

"Instinct. And the fact that it would have been very easy for you to have thrown suspicion on your husband just now. But you didn't. Let me know if you hear from him."

"I will."

After he left, I started shaking again. But this time it was with relief.

"DAVE'S CLEANERS WAS in the Cahills' driveway. I told the police that. I told them about you being parked at the Millers' too, Carrie. I had to. You can't withhold evidence, you know. It would've made me an accessory. It's not that I think you did it, you understand—

though, God knows, no one would blame you if you'd cut her head off . . ."

I was sitting at my desk in my home office going through my mail. I held the phone away from my ear as Sue Tomkins went through her litany. She wasn't one of my most favorite people. Over the years her efforts at friendship with me had increased in direct proportion to the success of Rich's business. It didn't surprise me that I hadn't heard word one from her since he left.

When she finally took a breath, I jumped in. "Sue, I appreciate your—uh—interest, but what I really need you to do is go over in your mind what you saw on Saturday. See if you can remember anything else."

"Why do you care? I should think you'd be out partying."

I kept my voice solemn. "Having a killer running around loose isn't my idea of a reason to celebrate."

I could tell from her silence that this was an angle she hadn't contemplated.

"I—I assumed it was a crime of passion directed at Erica," she murmured after a minute. "I hadn't considered the possibility there's some loony-tune out there."

"Well, just between you and me, that's the feeling in the department," I prevaricated conspiratorially. "I'm kind of working with the police, because I was there just a while before she was killed. They keep asking me if I saw anything unusual—you know, a car or something that didn't belong. You're such an observant person"—when all else fails, try flattery—"I thought you might have noticed something I missed."

"Dave's Cleaners. That's all I remember." Then, with a

note of suspicion in her voice: "How could you be working with the police? Aren't you . . ." She let it hang.

"What?"

"Well . . . a suspect?"

I forced a laugh. "C'mon, Sue, I may've hated Erica, but I'm no killer. The police know that."

"Really."

I held on to my temper. "I'm sure they'd appreciate any help you could give."

"Well, of course, but—"

I got creative. "If you helped break the case, I bet you'd get your picture in the paper. Who knows, they might even do an M.O.W.," I added, dropping some showbiz lingo I'd picked up.

"What's an M.O.W.?"

"Movie of the Week. TV people pay big money for these stories! 'Crime solved by a local housewife.' You know how they eat that sort of thing up."

There was silence on the other end of the line, and I let it linger.

"You know," she said after a very long pause, "I think I do remember something."

My heart stopped beating, then resumed an uneven *ta-dum, ta-dum, thump, thump, ta-dum.* "Yeah?"

"There was a car cruising the street."

"What do you mean, cruising?"

"You know, it went up and down the street a few times."

"You sure?" Maybe I'd painted too alluring a picture, and this was all a figment of Sue's greedy imagination. "How come you didn't tell the police about it?"

"I just thought of it. At the time it barely registered. I thought it was some guy looking for the Lambert kid. You know which one I mean, Paige—"

"She's away at college."

"So it couldn't've been for her!" Sue was caught up in it now. Her voice cracked with excitement. "I think I'm onto something. Maybe it was—"

"What'd the car look like?"

Long pause. "I think it was dark green. Or maybe black. It looked new."

"What make?"

"Hell, I don't know. One of those Japanese things— like a Nissan. Or an Acura."

"For God's sake, Sue, can't you tell an Acura from a Nissan?!"

"No, I can't! I buy American!"

I tried to repair the damage. "I didn't mean—"

"Maybe I'll just call that cop myself."

"Did you see who was driving?" I asked before she hung up on me. "A man or a woman?"

I could hear the wheels whirring in her head. Why should she share the glory, much less the movie rights, with me?

"A guy, I think," she muttered finally.

"Did it slow up in front of my—of Rich's house?"

"Didn't notice. That's all I can tell you, Carrie. Fang's crying at the door. I gotta take him for a walk."

Imagine naming that cream puff Fang. Damn, I was mad at myself. She'd shut down like a computer screen in a blackout. "Okay, Sue," I said, with false heartiness.

"You've been great. Knew I could count on you. Give me a call if anything else occurs to you, okay?"

"Yeah, sure," she responded unenthusiastically, and hung up.

I wondered what to do with the information. Maybe I should tell Brodsky, let him follow up on it. I was reaching for the phone when my eye fell on a familiar logo: *Arthur Carboni, Attorney at Law.*

A bill? I knew I still owed Arthur money, but I was paying him in installments, and I always paid him on the fifteenth. Why would he be sending me a bill now? Slitting open the envelope, I withdrew a neatly typed invoice for eighteen hundred and fifty dollars. Eighteen hundred! Where did that come from? I'd put down seventy-five hundred at the initial hiring, and he'd gone through that like Matt through a heavenly hash sundae! I studied the bill. Itemized, one hundred fifty for two phone calls, two hundred for my installment payment, and fifteen hundred for the services of an investigative firm called Mirimar, which Carboni had hired to look into Rich's finances. I scanned the page. For fifteen hundred dollars, these charlatans spent several days observing 101 Deerview Place and discovered that Rich was living with Erica there, noted that his office building actually did exist and that the sun was shining on the days the investigator visited it, searched the refuse bin outside the building and found it contained nothing incriminating, and after a visit to the hall of records, learned Rich had a mortgage of ninety thousand dollars left on the house. They'd also called his stockbroker, who had refused to disclose information on a client, and pulled his

TRW, coming up with the savvy conclusion that Rich was solvent and had no judgments against him. All of which they could have found out by asking me.

There was one eyestopper on the sheet: the investigator had followed Rich to a restaurant called Haji's Corner on MacDougal Street in Greenwich Village. He had watched Rich meet with an attractive young woman. No further description of the woman was given. The investigator had noted that they'd left separately. I was curious. Was it a business luncheon, or had Rich been cheating on Erica? Could this be important?

The report, except for this piece of information, was a rip-off. I went through it in detail, making note of the hours the investigator allegedly had spent over several days alternating between watching Rich's building and his home. I checked the dates; March 28 through April 12. The whole thing was a scam, I thought disgustedly. If Rich had hidden money, which I was sure he had, looking through his company garbage wasn't going to unearth it. And watching our house . . .

Suddenly, sunlight burst through a raincloud. If there had been a new dark-colored Acura or Nissan parked in Rich's lot or parked near the house at any of these times, surely a trained investigator would remember. Maybe, if we were really lucky, he'd have noted the license plate number. Mirimar had been no help in my getting a better settlement, but maybe, just maybe, they'd earned their fifteen hundred bucks after all.

WEDNESDAY
MAY 26

WEDNESDAY IS MY DAY off, which, as any working mother will tell you, means errand day. As soon as Allie and Matt left for school, I called Tina Moscone about switching car pools. Tina's one of those friends you make because your kids are in the same class and on the same Little League team, so you're driving the same car pools. We've worked on a couple of PTA committees together. She's easy to get along with, and I was pretty certain I could count on her.

"I'm sure everything'll be straightened out in a couple of weeks, Tina. I'll drive for you for a month if you'll cover me."

"Forget about making it up. Everybody has times they need a little help. Are you—is everything okay with you and the kids?"

"We're managing. But I don't want to be responsible for getting the children to school and practice and everything in case—anything comes up."

"No problem," she said, tactfully refraining from asking embarrassing questions. "Tell Allie and Matt they can come here if you're going to be late. Italians never run out of pasta."

"Thanks. I appreciate it."

I hung up, determined to get to know Tina better after all this was over.

A quick glance at the calendar showed a ten-thirty appointment at the vet's. All three cats were due to have their shots.

I had a moment of panic. I'd let them out this morning. God knew where they'd gone by now. I flew out of the house in my robe with Horton in pursuit. Placido was sunning himself on the front porch. I made a grab for him, but he took off like a cheetah who's spotted his dinner when Horton came charging out the door.

"Sit, Horty!" I yelled in frustration. But sitting was the last thing on Horton's mind. Whatever his ancestry, there is definitely no sheepdog.

Three-quarters of an hour later, with Horton safely locked inside the house, I'd rounded up the yowling trio, won the battle of the carrier cages, and lined them up on the front porch. Their ear-splitting complaints followed me into the house.

I telephoned Meg and asked her if she could get free for a few hours. I wanted moral support when I faced down the Mirimar investigator. She promised to arrange for Franny to relieve her by noon.

Good as his word, Brodsky had had my car delivered. It was parked in front of my house, the keys pushed through my mail slot, but I took Meg's car so I could return it.

As I backed out of the driveway, I was surprised to see Ruth-Ann standing at my curb putting something in my mailbox. She started almost guiltily when she saw me. I pulled to the top of the driveway and stopped the car.

"Looking for me, Ruth-Ann?"

"Yes . . . no, that is I—left something for you."

"Why didn't you come to the door and ring the bell?"

"I know today's your day off. I . . . thought you might be sleeping."

From the backseat came the protesting chorus. "Not with this family."

"Oh, you have cats!" She peered in through the window. "I love cats. How many have you got?"

"Three. On their way to the vet. And I'm afraid I'm late. What is it you have for me?"

She opened the mailbox and pulled out a newspaper

with a card attached. "It's the *Phoenix*," she whispered. "That reporter wrote a story about you."

I tried not to look, but my eyes refused to obey my brain's command. The headline struck me with the force of a whirlwind, sucking the breath from my body.

LOCAL LADY IN LURID LOVE LIAISON

A picture of my back as I'd scurried up the stairs to my office, with my name boldly printed under it, stared back at me. I could feel the heat creeping up my neck to the roots of my hair. "Throw it in the garbage, Ruth-Ann. I don't want to know what it says."

"I showed it to my uncle. That's his card. He's a lawyer. He says you could sue for defamation of character."

"I'm not suing anyone. No one I know reads that trash anyway." My breath was coming in short gasps. I couldn't bring myself to look at Ruth-Ann. "I'm really late. I have to go. Tell your uncle, thanks anyway."

I felt her hand on my arm, her voice soft, urgent. "You shouldn't let them get away with slandering you. You should fight back."

"I know you and your uncle mean well, and I appreciate it, really I do, but I don't have the time or the money to go up against the *Phoenix*. So please just forget about it. I'll see you in Group tomorrow."

And I took off as though pursued by all the tabloid photographers in the tristate area.

As I hit the accelerator, my foot came in contact with a hard object wedged between it and the brake pedal. Rattled by the headline and what I imagined was contained in the *Phoenix* article, I kicked it aside. It wasn't until I had driven through town and stopped at the stop sign on Broadway and Piermont Avenue that I tugged it loose and saw what it was. Dot's key ring must have fallen out of my pocket as I drove back to my office Monday afternoon. The light changed, and I tossed the keys onto the passenger seat.

The three girls who work in the office at the animal hospital all know me pretty well, but today they hardly glanced up from their computers.

"Hi," I faltered after I'd deposited the carriers on the bench. "I'm here for the cats' shots."

"Dr. Stoner'll be right with you, Mrs. Burnham," Holly replied without moving from her desk.

"Thanks," I muttered, and sat down on the hard bench next to my three loyal furry friends.

Dr. Stoner had nursed one or another of my four-legged family members through many a crisis, the last being a really mean eye infection José had contracted and passed on to his brothers. The vet was a jovial man of gargantuan proportions, with a touch as gentle as Florence Nightingale's. He took us right on schedule. The cats carried on as though they were being sent to the gas chamber.

"Blow in his face," Dr. Stoner instructed me as I struggled to keep a noisy, squirming Luciano on the slippery metal table.

"They're worse than usual today," I panted between breaths. "I don't know what's gotten into them."

"Animals're pretty sensitive. They pick up on tension they feel from their owners."

"Really?" I mumbled, resolved to show no emotion.

Dr. Stoner paused, needle in hand, and smiled at me. "You just hang in there. This'll all blow over before you know it."

My resolve crumbled like dry rot in the face of his kindness. "I feel like howling louder than Lucie. The girls in the office didn't even say hello."

"Nobody thinks you were involved. They're just uncomfortable. Probably didn't know what to say."

"You think that was it?"

"I'm sure it was," he said firmly, and plunged the needle into Luciano's rump.

As I was paying the bill, Judy, the plump assistant who's been with Dr. Stoner the longest, patted my hand and whispered, "I'm not one to wish anyone harm, but if you ask me, she deserved it."

DRIVING HOME TO drop off the cats, I kept thinking about Dot's keys. I remembered Brodsky saying Dot hadn't been home or at Rich's office. If she'd taken a few days off, this was the ideal time to search her apartment. By the time I pulled up in front of Meg's shop, my mind was made up. Mirimar could wait.

I could see Meg talking to a customer just inside the doorway. Impatient to get started, I leaned on the horn and waved. An eternity later she joined me, and I moved to the passenger seat.

"That was a two-hundred-dollar sale," she commented dryly as she shifted the car smoothly into gear. "You mind my asking what's so important that you couldn't let me write it up?"

I dangled the keys in front of her. "Change of plans. We're going to search Dot's apartment."

She shot me a look that said louder than words that she thought I'd flipped out. "With or without Dot in it?"

"She's not there. At least, I don't think she is. We'll have to phone first."

"Called breaking and entering, isn't it?"

"Not when you don't have to pick the lock."

"Aren't you in enough trouble? You have to go looking for it?"

"I am in trouble," I agreed. "That's why you've got to help me."

"Forget it. I'm not going to help you land yourself in jail."

"Meg," I pleaded, "Dot knows everything that goes on in that company."

"So what? What do you think you're going to find in her apartment, assuming you can get in and out without anyone seeing you? The murder weapon?"

"Maybe. If Dot killed Erica, there'll be something in that apartment that will give her away. She's not clever enough to cover her tracks completely."

The car slowed, and Meg angled in toward the curb. "I'm your friend," she said when she'd brought the car to a halt. "I'll go with you to Mirimar, I'll help you find a lawyer, I'll even go door to door and grill your old neighbors— even that Tomkins creature. But I refuse to go along with this insane idea of breaking into Dot's apartment. Clear?"

"Why're you being like this? What's the worst that can happen?"

"God, you're so naïve. The worst that can happen is you get arrested, you get convicted, you do time, and you have a record for the rest of your life! How would you like to explain that to your kids?"

"How do you suggest I explain a murder rap to them?" I countered coldly.

She didn't answer, just reached into her purse for a cigarette. We sat there in silence, the tension like a wall between us. She smoked and I fumed. I knew she was adamant. I'd touched a chord somewhere, and nothing I could say or do was going to change her mind.

After a moment I came up with another idea. "Would you go into New York with me?"

"I thought we were going to talk to the investigator."

"That can wait. There's someone I want to talk to first."

"Who?"

"Don't worry. I plan to ring his bell like a good law-abiding citizen."

"Well, that's a plus. Anybody I know?"

"Guy used to work for Rich. Erica forced him to resign. Name's Herb Golinko."

W E FOUND HERB in Saint Claire's Hospital in Manhattan, on an AIDS floor. When I phoned Herb's house, I got his live-in lover, who gave me the news.

In all the years I'd known Herb, I'd never discussed anything other than company business with him. I knew nothing about his personal life except that he'd been wounded in the Korean war. I hadn't been aware he was gay. I don't think anyone in the company had either, because Erica would surely have used it against him.

"I think I would've preferred breaking into Dot's apartment," Meg announced glumly as we drove down Ninth Avenue looking for a parking space.

"I know," I agreed. "I feel terrible bothering him when he's so sick."

"How long's he been in the hospital?"

"Charles didn't say, and I didn't ask."

"How bad is he?"

"Charles was crying."

"Jesus." Meg turned down Fifty-first Street and found an empty meter. We didn't talk while she concentrated on backing into the tight space without creaming the car behind us. After she turned off the motor, she sat staring at an ambulance parked near the hospital emergency entrance. "You sure we should go ahead with this?" she asked finally. "You don't really think he did it, do you?"

"I guess he couldn't have if he's been in the hospital."

"Right. So . . ."

"On the other hand, if he wasn't, he wouldn't have had anything to lose, would he?"

Meg sighed and opened the door. "Let's go."

THE HOSPITAL RECEPTION area was a microcosm of New York City's unmelted ethnic pot. We took our place at the end of a line of impatient visitors waiting to

91

be given the thumbs-up by a supercilious receptionist ensconced behind a large wraparound desk. There was no air conditioning. Despite the improved temperature outside, by the time our turn came, I looked like I'd been caught in a rainstorm. Fortunately for us, visiting hours were in progress, and we were given passes without much hassle. The receptionist did cast a suspicious glance at Meg, who had the appearance of a woman who'd just taken a cool shower. There are some people to whom dirt, grime, and sweat simply do not adhere.

We followed a yellow line down a narrow corridor to an elevator bank and waited ten minutes for it to arrive. By the time we reached Herb's floor, I was bedraggled in spirit as well as body and dreading the coming interview.

Herb shared a room with three other men, all similarly afflicted. Not one glanced up as we entered their space.

I hardly recognized Herb. He'd lost at least thirty pounds; you could see every bone. The black eye patch stood out starkly against his pallor, and the veins in his hands were so close to the surface, his skin looked azure-blue against the white coverlet. Would this man have had the energy to lift a rock, much less bash Erica's head in with it? I glanced at Meg and knew by her expression that our thoughts were running along similar lines.

"Herb?" I kept my voice to a whisper. It seemed sacrilegious to speak normally here.

He opened his eye, turned his head listlessly in my direction, didn't recognize me immediately. "Carrie?"

"Hi, Herb."

"What the hell're you doing here?"

"I . . . came to see you."

He took in Meg, then raised himself slightly. "Rich with you?"

"No. He—uh . . . you didn't know we're separated?"

"Can't say I'm surprised."

Had everyone known about Erica but me? I felt Meg's comforting grip on my arm.

"I spoke to Charles today. That's how I knew you were here." I shifted uneasily, wondering how I was going to lead into the reason for my visit.

"Who's your friend?" he asked finally.

"Sorry. This is Meg Reilly."

Meg pulled up a chair and nervously took out a cigarette. She dropped the pack on the chair and held out her hand. "Hi."

He took it with his fragile one. "Spare a butt?"

Meg reached for the pack. "Sure."

I was horrified. "Meg, this is a hospital. You can't—"

"What the hell's the difference?" she hissed at me.

Herb smiled for the first time. "I'll be discreet."

Meg placed a Marlboro between his lips and lit it. Herb took a drag, seemed to gather energy, and struggled to a sitting position.

"Okay, Carrie, what's this about? You didn't suddenly get a calling to visit the sick and wounded, did you?"

I was embarrassed and ashamed, but I was here, so I forged ahead. "I came to see you about Erica Vogel. I wondered if you knew—"

He choked and started coughing. Meg took the cigarette from his shaking hand.

"That witch!" he managed when the spasm subsided. "Got hers finally, didn't she?"

Meg handed him back the cigarette. "Sure did. How'd you know about it?"

"Charles called me."

"He tell you she was living with Rich—that it happened at my old house?" I asked.

He seemed startled. "No. But we didn't talk long. I was at my mom's when he called." He grimaced. "We don't talk long when I'm there. She hates Charles. Thinks this is his fault."

"You weren't here on Saturday?"

"Came in yesterday. They carted me here from the Cheshire Cheese." A crooked smile appeared briefly. "Caused quite a stir. A few diners permanently lost their appetites along with their soup."

"Then you were in New Jersey on Saturday," I said casually.

His laugh racked his wasted body more painfully than the cough. "Think I did it, Carrie. That it?"

"No!" I said uncomfortably, "of course not. Well . . ." All of a sudden honesty seemed the only way to go. "To tell the truth, I thought about it. Wouldn't've blamed you either, but I don't really think you have it in you. Any more than I do."

"So why're you here?"

"I—I'm a suspect, Herb."

His body started to shake underneath the covers, and I glanced around for the nurse before I realized he was laughing again.

"What a fucking joke," he gasped. "David vanquishing Goliath."

I didn't know whether to be insulted or flattered by the analogy. "Well, it wasn't this David. I was hoping you'd have some ideas about who else wasn't too fond of Erica."

"Maybe it was a burglar."

"Nothing was stolen." I didn't mention the necklace, but there was no reaction. I breathed easier.

He sank back onto his pillows and closed his eyes. "Could've been almost anyone. 'Let 'em eat shit' was her motto. Just rolled over anyone got in her way."

I knew.

"Everybody thought you knew about her. Just put up with it 'cause you liked livin' high. I told 'em you never knew about any of 'em. You were blind where he was concerned."

I felt like I'd been jabbed with a cattle prod. " 'Any of them'?"

"Carrie, let's go," Meg said, getting to her feet. "Herb needs his rest."

"Oh, Christ almighty, Carrie, sonofabitch's been chasin' every model walked through our doors for years. Just never took any of 'em seriously till her. What the hell was the matter with you?" Suddenly he was shouting. "What'd you think he was doing all those nights he said he was workin' late?"

His anger made him cough again. Meg took the cigarette and put it out. I couldn't speak. The three men in the other beds had turned off their TVs; we were better than the afternoon lineup of soaps.

"Always liked you," Herb continued, his voice soft again. "Pissed me off, how a smart lady like you could be so dumb about a man. Christ, it was a disease with him. Even that misbegotten gargoyle he calls a secretary!"

All of a sudden I felt nauseous. "Dot?" I croaked. "Dot Shea?"

"Visiting hours are now over" came over the loudspeaker. *"All visitors please leave the floors. Visiting hours are now over. . . ."*

"Ten years, baby," he hissed. "Ten fuckin' years that broad's been trailin' after him. Joke's on her, his leaving you for Erica. But she's been laughing at you—givin' you the finger. Hell, where were your eyes?"

The room blurred. Herb's words pounded in my ears. *"Every model who walked through our doors! Misbegotten gargoyle he calls a secretary. Ten years, baby! Ten fucking years!"*

Meg had to drag me to the elevator. My breathing was coming in jagged painful gasps as I leaned against the wall in the corridor.

The door to the elevator opened. I knew there were people in it, but I was hardly aware of them. We rode down in silence. Memories flashed through my mind. Images of Rich in his office talking to young hopefuls. Images of him with Dot the hundreds of times I saw them together, her eyes worshipping him, his, remote and businesslike. God, he was good at it. Did it make his infidelity worse knowing for certain there were many instead of just one? I wasn't sure. But by the time we got to the car, a kind of calm had settled over me. I was certain of what I was going to do. Meg knew it too.

"Oh, Carrie," she said. "Don't go off the deep end

because of what Herb said. He's so sick, who knows if he even knows what—"

"With or without you," I interrupted icily. "She had a motive. If there's anything in that goddamned apartment of hers, I'm going to find it." I turned away from her and stared out the window.

Cars flew by, white cars, green ones, blue, black . . . blue. I turned to Meg. "Who makes Integra?" I asked her.

She took her eyes off the road for a second and looked at me. "Acura. Why?"

I wanted to smile, but my lips wouldn't stretch that far. "Because I just remembered. A couple of months ago, Dot bought a new car. A blue one. A dark blue Acura Integra."

I TALKED MEG into stopping at a 7-Eleven so I could call Dot's apartment. The phone rang a dozen or more times. Dot was the only person I knew who didn't have an answering machine. Maybe because, if she wasn't in the office, she was almost always home. By now, I'd convinced myself she and Rich had gone off somewhere together. Some secret place—a love nest where they'd been rendezvousing monthly, or weekly, or maybe daily for the past ten years. Dot Shea! Neurotic, unsexy, born-again Dot! Erica—you could attribute her to a middle-age crisis. You could hate her, convince yourself she'd stolen him away by casting some magical, youthful spell. But Dot . . .

Stop! I told myself. This was old ground, covered months before in my therapist's office. What difference, at this point, if Rich got it on with one woman or a thousand? Some men are born womanizers. It's a known personality disorder.

But this was *my* husband who had been leading a double life right under my anesthetized nose. I had not only been blind, I must have been brain-dead.

Meg glanced at me inquiringly as I jumped in the passenger seat. "Well?"

"Not home."

"You still determined to go?"

"You don't have to come."

"Oh, shut up." She hit the accelerator, and we turned onto River Road.

D OT'S APARTMENT COMPLEX was located south of us in Edgewater, a town where high-rise buildings have sprung up like giant trees amid the weeds of commercial flotsam adjacent to the river. The town's proximity to New York City and its panoramic view of the Hudson had enticed developers out to make a quick buck to erect buildings wherever they could purchase land. Little if any thought was given to architectural harmony or to the original character of the town. The result was, the town had no character at all.

Dot's building, lacking a swimming pool and a health club, fell just short of being labeled luxurious. It did, however, have a doorman plus a security guard, who roamed the parking lot checking bumpers and windshields for tenants' and visitors' stickers.

Meg pulled over half a block from the entrance. "How're we going to get past the M.P.?"

A dilemma.

"If we park here," I said, "and walk along the river to the entrance, I think we can bypass him. We'll only have to deal with the doorman."

Meg flipped open her purse, applied some lipstick, and fluffed up her hair. "No problem," she replied, opening her door.

I didn't question her. I'd seen men preen like peacocks doing a courtship dance over Meg.

We jogged along a dirt road toward the river, residents out for our daily constitutional.

"You'll have to go up by yourself," Meg said.

"Wouldn't it be quicker if we both——?"

"I've got to keep the doorman's eyes off the elevator TV. Don't make me do it for longer than fifteen or twenty minutes."

"That won't give me enough time."

"Make it enough. We don't know where Dot's gone. She could come home any minute. Know her apartment number?"

I did. Fourteen K. I'd been there only once, when Dot first moved in several years before. She threw a party for herself celebrating her tenth year with the company. Rich groused and grumbled all the way over in the car, but once there, he was charm personified.

The doorman was a swarthy, Middle Eastern guy wearing a snappy blue uniform with gold buttons and a mustache that took up half his face.

I loitered among the rhododendron bushes watching in awe as Meg spun her web.

"Hi," I heard her say in a tone I hardly recognized. "Would you know if there are any apartments coming available in this building?"

"You must call real estate agency," the man replied. "I cannot give out this information."

"Oh." Meg looked forlorn, Cinderella barred from the ball. "It's just I'm in such a mess." Tears rolled out of those gorgeous eyes and trickled down her cheeks.

I was fascinated. *How the hell does she do that on cue?*

"I just broke up with my boyfriend," Meg sniffled. "It's his apartment, and he's got a new girlfriend. She's moving in next week. I've got to find something right away."

"I give you number to call." The man started toward his little office with Meg following. "Not supposed to give out information, but seven N told me they find bigger place. Maybe you can sublet."

"I can't tell you how much I appreciate your going to all this trouble for somebody you don't even know." Meg's smile would have defrosted Saddam Hussein.

The doorman's answering smile became a leer. "Must be very strange man, your boyfriend, not want a sexy lady like you."

I didn't hear how Meg dealt with that; they had moved out of my line of vision.

Good goin', Meggie, I thought as I made my way to the elevator bank.

My next thought, as I wiped my sweaty hands on my pants, was how I'd hate to have to do this for a living.

Pressing fourteen, my finger almost slipped off the button. Suddenly my nervousness went to my bladder. I jiggled from one foot to the other as the elevator stopped at the eighth floor. A woman with pure white hair and a disagreeable expression, pushing a loaded laundry cart, got on and frowned at me as we continued our ascent.

"Isn't this going down?"

"No," I mumbled, averting my face. "Up. Sorry."

The door opened, and I slipped past her. I didn't move toward Dot's apartment until I heard the elevator door shut behind me. She could be someone Dot knew. If they ever got to talking . . .

Paranoid. There was no way Dot could ever find out I'd been here.

Responding to a faint wisp of memory, I turned left down the hallway, glanced at the letters on the doors. H, I, J, K. K for kept woman . . .

I rang the bell just to be sure. Waited. Rang again, the key ring clutched so tightly in my hand, it left an imprint. What if Dot opened the door? I hadn't prepared a script. Minutes passed. Meg had advised me to stay no more than fifteen minutes, and I'd already used up a third of my allotment.

The first key I tried slid into the lock, but the door swung inward before I'd turned the knob. Trembling, I located a light switch by the hall mirror and flipped it on. What could have been the sitting area of a motel suite sprang into focus.

Off-white walls, matching walnut veneer tables, mattress-ticking-striped couch and lounge chair covered in plastic,

arranged in an L. Pathologically neat, impersonal, unimagi-
native. I had no memory of the decor from the party, except
that the couch looked familiar. I'd probably spent the entire
evening stuck to the plastic.

I walked around, searching for something to search. No
bookshelves, no desk, no chest of drawers, no buffet, nothing to open. I glanced into the combination kitchen–dining
room, was about to look in the cabinets, when I was again
seized with an undeniable urge.

I remembered that the only bathroom was off Dot's bedroom. I made a dash for it, tripped over something lying in
the entranceway, cursed as I fell, and felt a stinging in my
hand. Scrambling to my feet, I stumbled into the bedroom,
stopped. Not neat. Chaos. Dresser drawers open, contents
scattered. Closet doors ajar. Clothing strewn everywhere.
Sheets and blankets jerked from the bed, lying in rumpled
heaps amid splinters of glass.

My first impulse was to turn and run. The second was
to find a phone and call the police. No. How would I
explain my presence?

The crunching sound under my shoes focused my
attention on the hundreds of glass shards littering the rug.
It was as though a tornado had flown in through the
window and randomly trashed every picture in the place,
leaving untouched the large-screen television and the
bookshelf filled with paperback novels, as if they lay outside the storm's path.

Picture hooks indicated that the room had been wall-
to-wall pictures, framed photographs now lying smashed
on the carpet.

This was no normal break-in.

I bent down and picked up a broken frame. And froze. Rich looked back at me from a blowup of a photo I remembered as having been taken for the company's annual report. Knife slashes mutilated his face.

I saw blood on the picture! Panic swept over me as, for one moment of dementia, I thought the picture was bleeding. Then I realized the blood must be coming from my own hand.

Another picture. Rich again, this one an enlargement of a snapshot taken at a company Christmas party. Slashed. Rich and me at Dot's party. I'd been cut out of this photo before the mutilation took place. Another enlarged snap of Rich, standing by the building next to his logo. Cut to ribbons.

Was this Dot's handiwork? A woman gone over the brink, so consumed with jealousy, she had desecrated her own home?

Heedless now of the debris that tore at my knees, I crawled over to get a closer look at a stack of photos lying by an open bureau drawer, all of which seemed to be professional headshots of young beautiful women. The photographs separated in my hands, leaving me clutching torn half-faces. Familiar faces.

There was more blood on these. I looked at my hand. The blood had congealed. The bleeding had stopped. The blood on the pictures wasn't coming from me!

I was trapped in a horror movie. Run! Get out! Get downstairs to Meg!

I was shaking like a cornered animal when I reached

the door, but something—maybe it was that urge most of us have to gawk at disaster scenes, compelled me to take a last look. And I saw, coming from under the bathroom door, a tiny trickle. Barely aware I was moving in the wrong direction, I propelled myself back through the sea of glass, my feet pulverizing it, the sound augmented like a drumroll in my ears. Dazed, I pushed open the door.

Water dripped over the tub rim, puddling on the gray tile floor, berry juice canals winding across the room to the door.

I thought she was alive. Injured but alive. Naked, she lay half in, half out of the bathtub, eyes wide open. She moved! Suppressing a scream, I started forward. Much later I would be told the draft created when I opened the door had probably disturbed the water, causing her body to sway.

A hand, gashed as though attacked by a vicious animal, hung over the side of the tub, a mottled purplish look to the fingers. Her hair had come unpinned, was hanging disheveled around her shoulders, bleached by the fluorescent lighting to a mustard yellow. Her face, the color of wax, had taken on its texture. Congealed blood streaking from her nose, food protruding from her mouth . . . no! God, no, not food! Her tongue!

Then I saw the stab wounds on her chest.

And felt myself falling . . .

WAS CURLED up on the jail-striped couch. The room was teeming with strangers babbling incomprehensible things in loud voices that hurt my head. I looked up. Meg was holding my hand, murmuring comforting noises.

Someone was standing in a doorway to my right, taking photographs of another room. Someone else was dusting for fingerprints. I turned my head and saw a dark-skinned man in a doorman's uniform who kept wiping his forehead with the back of his sleeve and glancing in Meg's direction as he talked to a policeman. I was trying to remember where I'd seen him when a glowering Ted Brodsky, jacket off, shirt collar open, walked around the photographer and over to the doorman.

I sat bolt upright. "Oh God," I moaned. "Oh, shit, oh, God! Meg, Meggie, Dot's dead! Dot's—someone—oh, God!"

Meg wrapped her arms around me and rocked me. "I know, honey, I know."

The hostile look Brodsky cast my way when he heard my voice made me squeeze my eyes shut again and pray to the God who had clearly deserted me that I might keep them closed forever.

I couldn't. I could feel Brodsky's stare boring right through my eyelids, willing them to open.

"Take it easy, Carrie," Meg said, gently pushing me back down. "Don't try to talk."

A wave of nausea began its upward journey. I fought it, and it passed. I had a bizarre urge to feign amnesia and wail, "Where am I?" in my best Sarah Bernhardt voice, but the expression on Brodsky's face made it clear histrionics wouldn't fly.

"Well, Ms. Carlin," he said, taking two giant steps that

landed him beside the couch. "You sure have a penchant for being in the wrong place at the wrong time."

He wasn't calling me Carrie anymore.

"Your friend filled me in on what brought you here. What happened after you broke into the apartment?"

"I didn't break in!"

"Cut the crap."

"I had a key."

His eyes raked me. "The lock's been forced."

"It was open when I got here." I was trying desperately to piece together the events of the last hour. One thing, though, was depressingly apparent. It was happening again. I was involved in another murder. My heart started hammering, doing its best to break out of my chest.

What had happened after I found Dot? How had Meg gotten here? Who had called the police? Meg saw my confusion.

"I panicked when you didn't come down after half an hour. And I was having a bitch of a time keeping Ali Baba there at bay. I made him bring me up, and we—we found you and . . . her—in the bathroom. Damn you, Carrie"—her voice broke—"for a minute I thought you were dead too." She took a breath and her voice steadied. "Doorman called 911."

Brodsky pulled a chair next to the couch and sat. "I want to know step by step what you did after you got in this apartment," he said coldly. "Did you and Ms. Shea have an argument?"

I stared at him blankly. "An argument? How could I?

She was dead! At first I thought—but then I saw her—she was dead!"

"I don't think you should question her now," Meg said, giving my shoulder a warning squeeze. "Anyone can see she's not—"

Brodsky swung on her angrily. "Back off."

Meg stood her ground. "If you're going to accuse her of anything, she should be read her rights, she should have a lawyer present."

Accuse me! I know how a rabbit gone to ground feels when he sees the fox's nose at the only exit. I started to shake.

"Goddammit, you want to talk charges?" I'd never seen Brodsky so furious. "Let's put murder one aside for now. Let's start with breaking and entering. A crime, lady, which you were an accessory to."

"Oh, for chrissake, she'd just found out that pig of a husband of hers had been making it with Dot Shea for years. We thought maybe there'd be something here to prove—"

Meg stopped midsentence, suddenly aware she was providing the police with a perfect motive for my killing Dot.

Brodsky ignored it. "You thought!" he exploded. "Well, you were wrong, weren't you? Why can't you and your lunatic friend here leave the detective work to the detectives? We're paid to put our asses on the line."

"We weren't wrong!" I cried out. It was all coming back. I remembered the broken glass, the torn pictures— The words came tumbling out.

"I mean, we were wrong about Dot being the killer, but

we weren't wrong about finding something here. She's turned that bedroom into a . . . a temple. A shrine to Rich. She had pictures of him all over the place. Snapshots she'd had enlarged and framed." I paused for breath. "And I think whoever killed her might go after him next because all of the pictures were smashed and they all had knife slashes through his face."

"That wasn't you?" Brodsky's voice was flat.

Suddenly rage overcame terror, and I was yelling at the top of my voice. "For God's sake, I was only here for a few minutes! I'm not Superwoman! I didn't kill Dot, and I didn't rip the pictures of those girls in half either, and I didn't bleed all over them."

I had his attention now. "What pictures?"

"These, Lieutenant." A detective, carefully holding the photos by the edges, set the pile on the coffee table. They were jumbled together so that the halves didn't match up. "Found them scattered by the bureau."

"That's Jeanine Gray!" I almost shouted, pointing to one lovely face that still had an intact nose. "Rich used her for a lipstick spread. And this"—I pointed to another with a blood smear across the cheek—"this is Helga Swenson. Meg, remember my telling you about her?"

Meg, her face white, reached out to pick up the pictures.

"Don't touch," Brodsky warned, stopping her hands.

Just then the door to the bedroom opened. I looked up in time to see Dot's corpse, in a body bag, wheeled out into the hall. The dizziness I'd been battling dimmed the room, and I must have made some sound because I felt strong hands push my head down between my knees and heard Brodsky's voice, surprisingly gentle now, telling me to take deep breaths. Minutes later I was pushed back onto the couch, and I felt hands placing a wet cloth on my forehead. From somewhere in outer space, I heard Brodsky telling Meg to take me home as soon as I was feeling well enough. "Stay with her overnight if you can. I'll stop by tomorrow."

Later, Meg helped me up, and we made our way past the detective dusting for fingerprints, to the elevator. I prayed that the killer had been careless—that mine wouldn't be the only prints he lifted.

M EG STAYED OVER.

She told Matt and Allie I wasn't feeling well and let me soak in the tub while she whipped up dinner. I didn't have to face my children until their stomachs were full and they'd been given the bare facts about the day's events.

"Where could Dad be, Mom?" Matt wanted to know. "Why doesn't he call?"

"I don't know, honey. But I'm sure he's okay." I was amazed that the words came out of my mouth actually sounding coherent.

"How do you know?" Allie quavered.

If Rich was all right, he wasn't going to be when I got through with him. What was I supposed to tell my children? I believe in honesty. Fantasies can be worse than reality.

"Well, I don't really know for sure, Allie," I replied finally. "You have to remember, Dad's in shock. He probably just wanted to be by himself for a while. When he hears about—about today, he'll show up."

Meg herded them upstairs and, incredibly, got them started on homework. Then we sat in the living room, and while I absently stroked Placido, we decided on a course of action.

"You've got to talk to a lawyer," Meg said.

"I know. Tomorrow I'm going to call this guy I went to college with. I just came across his name."

"You aren't going to call one of the lawyers I told you about?"

"I thought I'd try Steve first. He always liked me. Maybe he'll give me a break, price wise."

"Forget the money! I'll lend you the money!"

I squeezed her hand. "Thanks, but I think I should give this a shot."

"But you can't hire just anybody! This is too serious. You need somebody really top."

"He's not just anybody. His name's Steve Ehrlich, of Ehrlich, Ehrlich, & Greenspan. I read in the paper that he and his brother recently defended somebody in the Mafia and got him off."

"Oh well, what better recommendation."

"At least I know him. Every time I talk to Arthur, I hear the meter ticking. He makes me feel as if I'm just part of his car payment. Steve always liked me. I'll be more comfortable dealing with him than a stranger."

"How do you know he's any good? Just because—"

"How do I know those other lawyers are good?"

"Because I got their names from a reliable source."

"What reliable source?"

Meg concentrated on pulling a loose thread through the sleeve of her sweater and did what she always did when I got personal. Avoiding answering. And capitulated.

"Do what you think best, then," she said. "If this guy's firm represents Mafia types, they must be sharp."

It wasn't exactly the kind of company I wanted to be keeping, but she had a point.

I was about to pursue the subject of her "reliable source" when the brandy I'd been sipping hit me like a tranquilizer dart. I lay back and closed my eyes.

"Go on up to bed," Meg said. "I'll see to the kids."

What does it matter who her sources are? I thought wearily as I tucked Placido under my arm and climbed the stairs to my bedroom. *I don't care if her reliable source is Jack the Ripper. All that matters is she's a damned good friend, and I'm lucky to have her.*

Not bothering to dislodge Horton from where he lay sprawled across the bottom half of my bed, I curled into a fetal position, and drifted off.

I'm standing on a flimsy rope bridge strung over a deep chasm, trying to reach something on the other side—a large round shimmering object partially obscured in shadow. Below me the swirling water is angry. I hear its roar as it smashes against the rocks. The rope is fraying, but every time I start to cross the bridge, it sways, forcing me back. I'm terrified I'll fall into the abyss below. The thing floats away before I am halfway across.

T H U R S D A Y
MAY 27

THE GRAFFITI DEFACING the buildings on the Henry Hudson Parkway always depress me. I'm old enough to remember a time when New York City's streets were relatively free of garbage and the walls of the buildings looked like walls of buildings, not blackboards in a metropolitan jungle. I tried to focus on the New Jersey skyline across the river as I drove. Once in town, I deliberately bypassed the Fifty-seventh Street turn-off, where the windshield cleaners armed with filthy brushes lay in wait. I took the Fifty-fourth Street exit.

Steven Ehrlich's office was on Fifty-fifth and the Avenue of the Americas in the MGM building. I spent twenty minutes looking for a parking space and ended up in a garage that charges ten dollars for the first hour.

I'd gotten right through to Steve when I'd called his office early that morning. He remembered me and sounded pleased to hear from me. I'd told him only that I was in trouble, I needed professional advice, and he fit me right in. We'd made an appointment for eleven.

I had dressed carefully, even putting a few rollers in my hair in an attempt to give it the bounce it used to have when I was in college. I selected a royal blue linen suit that accentuates my eyes and in which I've always felt attractive. Today it hung loosely, and I had to pin in the waistband. It fit me the way Ted Brodsky's clothes fit him. Maybe we had something in common. We both lost weight under stress. Briefly, I wondered if his stress was job-related or if there was another reason.

I arrived at Steve's office breathless, with less than a minute to spare.

The reception area reeked of success. I recognized a prominent television actor's photograph on the wall, with a little note appended above his autograph, thanking Dan and Steve Ehrlich and their dedicated staff for "their competence, friendship and support." A ficus was blooming happily in an antique oriental planter near the window. My two-inch heels almost drowned in the mauve carpet. I decided Steve was doing very well indeed. Chances were I couldn't afford him.

When the receptionist announced me, Steve bounded out of his office and threw his arms around me.

"Carrie! Little Carrie Carlin." My feet dangled above the carpet as he whirled me around. "What a wonderful surprise, hearing your voice after all these years."

"I—I—it's great seeing you too, Steve." He put me down, and flustered, I fussed with my hair and patted it back into place.

Steve isn't what you'd call handsome or sexy. He's a little on the pudgy side and has a slight overbite. When we were in school, he'd had a crush on me, but his mouth always reminded me of Bugs Bunny. I'd never felt inclined to kiss it. Still, he has a nice face—one of those freckled little-boy-cherubic visages that never seem to grow older. I could see where that would stand him in good stead in a courtroom. What jury would vote against Bugs Bunny?

Arm around my shoulder, he led me into his office, as elegant as, if more understated than, the reception area. He sat next to me on the soft green leather sofa instead of taking a seat behind his burled walnut desk.

"How long has it been? Fifteen years? You've hardly changed."

I tried to smile. It was more like eighteen years, and I felt as though I'd aged an additional ten in the past five days.

"What's the matter, Carrie?" he inquired with such

concern on his round face, two big tears escaped and rolled down my cheeks.

Shit, I thought, digging in my pocket for a tissue. One word of kindness from any source, and I leak like a washerless faucet.

Steve was a good listener. He didn't interrupt as I recounted the extraordinary events of the past week. As I spoke, he made notes on a legal pad.

"I read about the Vogel murder, but I didn't connect the name Burnham with you."

"I wish I hadn't connected the name Burnham with me!"

He patted my hand sympathetically. "You've had a bad time, but it's going to get better."

He was as nice as I'd remembered, and I found myself opening up. "The worst of it is, I loved Rich. I never saw it coming. Until that last year I really believed we had something special."

"His loss. You're a special lady."

Now why couldn't I have fallen for this guy when I had the chance?

"Stop," I murmured. "You'll start me blubbering."

"I have a broad shoulder."

"What I need is your legal expertise."

He hesitated. "How are you left financially?"

Uh-oh. My eyes wandered to the Lichtenstein hanging over his desk. "I'm managing. I used to work mornings at a pain center, but a few months after Rich left I started my own practice. Rich hasn't been bad about money. He's agreed to pay alimony for several years, and he's responsible for child support till Matt and Allie are through college. It's not like when we were married, of course, but—"

"Come on," Steve said, holding out his hand and rising. "Let's have lunch and work out a strategy."

"You're going to represent me?" I could feel Atlas' globe being lifted off my shoulders.

He squeezed my hand. "Of course. We alums have to stick together."

Involuntarily, I glanced at his left hand, noted he wasn't wearing a wedding band. I glanced at his desk. There was a framed photograph of a pretty smiling woman and two little girls. So much for the fleeting thought.

"Maybe . . . we should discuss your fee first."

I knew this was sticky ground. He was a partner in a firm. Even if he wanted to give me a break, I wasn't sure he had the authority to do it.

"I get four hundred dollars an hour."

I blanched. He might as well have said a thousand. "I'm afraid I can't. . . ."

"Don't worry. We'll work something out."

I flashed him a suspicious look but saw only friendly concern in his eyes.

We lunched at Sushiden, a pricey Japanese restaurant on East Forty-ninth Street. The ambience, Steve's warmth, the sake all combined to make me feel as though someone had slid little fur muffs over my frazzled nerve endings. We talked about normal things—college, professors, class-mates we remembered; we traded anecdotes about

clients—we'd both had our share of kooks over the years—
and our children; we both had two.

"I've always missed having a son," Steve remarked as
the waitress was bringing our green tea. "You're lucky you
have one of each."

"You can't make me feel sorry for you," I said.
"Everyone knows daughters dote on their daddies. You've
got three beautiful women spoiling you rotten."

He covered my hand with his. "Only two, I'm afraid.
Lenore and I—well, things aren't the way they used
to be."

The fur muffs started shredding around the edges. I
focused on my sushi. "I really love this stuff. Haven't had
it in a while, though. My kids aren't into raw—"

"We've grown apart over the years. You know how
it is."

Clang, clang went the warning bells, "No," I said.
"Tell me."

"It's not Len. Believe me, I don't have a bad word to say
about her, but our lives have gone in different directions."

"In what way?"

"I think she's come to hate what I do. When I was rep-
resenting Tony the Toad, there were nights I was literally
afraid to go home." He grinned that rabbit grin. "And it
wasn't the mob I was afraid of."

"I seem to remember in college and law school you
were really gung ho about putting the mob behind bars.
Whatever happened to all that idealism?"

"I was a kid. I've changed. Shit happens, you know?"

I certainly did. I knew all about shit. The hum of the

other patrons receded as I flashed back to Rich's words to me that last night.

"It's not you," he'd mumbled miserably. *"You haven't done anything. It's me. Shit happens. People change."*

I looked across the table at Steve. His soft brown eyes had gone beady, his buck teeth grown to monster proportions. "I liked that kid," I said, reaching for my handbag.

"I always had a thing for you too, Carrie." His hand dropped to my thigh.

I slapped it away as though it was a crawling bug. "You should think hard about what you're doing. Divorce is a nightmare."

He looked shocked. "Who said anything about divorce?"

"Oh, I see. Fooling around's okay, though."

"What's the big deal? No one has to get hurt."

"Except your wife when she finds out. And your kids. And the kid you used to be." I got to my feet. "Thanks for lunch."

"Oh, lighten up, Car. You know as well as I do, a little hanky-panky holds more marriages together than you women want to admit."

Wrong buttons! I controlled an urge to pour the green tea down his pants. "You think getting some Mafia sleazebag off makes you hot stuff, don't you?" I said. "The truth is, it really makes you no better than he is. You're just cheating the system like you've cheated your wife!" People were staring. My voice went up a decibel. "And if you're going to cheat, at least have the guts to call it what it is. Hanky-panky is so high school."

I walked out of the restaurant.

ONCE OUT OF the city I opened the windows and let the fresh spring air clear my head. I has glad I'd spoken my piece. In retrospect I decided I'd deserved what I'd gotten for considering hiring a Mafia lawyer in the first place. Fortunately, I had Meg's recommendations in reserve. I made a mental note to call her.

The evening was going to be a busy one. I'd canceled my morning appointments, planning to start at four and work till eight or nine. Most of my patients had been cooperative about rescheduling. No one had brought up the murders. Maybe, like that slimebucket Steve, they hadn't made the connection. I'd arranged for the kids to have dinner with friends, scheduled my overeaters from four to five-thirty, planned a half hour for dinner, had one patient coming at six and one at seven. No one at eight. Vickie came to mind. I'd forgotten to call her about scheduling another appointment and decided to go for the extra phone charges. Maybe she could fill that eight o'clock slot. When a line opened up, I dialed her number. She answered on the first ring.

"Vickie? It's Carrie Carlin."

"Hi."

"I have an opening at eight tonight. Is that good for you?"

"Gosh, I don't know. I'm going for a job interview in the morning."

"No kidding. That's terrific!" Vickie had never held a job for longer than two months. Her interpersonal relationship skills were weak, and she was unreliable, sometimes arriving at work late, at times not showing up at all. Brain-wave training for attention would help, but we weren't there yet. We were still working on positive affirmations and visualizations. "What kind of a job is it?"

"A friend got me an interview at Bloomingdale's."

"As a salesgirl?"

"Demonstrating makeup."

"Hey, that's great. You have such beautiful eyes. You'll be perfect. Good luck."

"Thanks. I am kind of nervous."

"Why don't you try and make it tonight, then? We'll go over interviewing strategies, do a success visualization."

"Okay."

"Good. See you later."

"Yeah. 'Bye."

" 'Bye." I hung up feeling better. I was making progress with Vickie. This job, if she could get and keep it, would give her a degree of independence. Maybe she'd move out of her parents' home.

It was therapeutic, getting my mind off my problems and concentrating on those of my patients.

I reached for the phone again and dialed Meg's shop.

Franny's voice. "Meg's Place."

"Franny?"

"How may I help you?"

"It's Carrie. What're you doing there today? Where's Meg?"

"Oh, Carrie." Her voice became hushed. "Meg had to leave."

"On a Thursday at lunch hour? Where'd she go?"

"A couple of policemen came by. I don't know what it was about, but they asked her to go to the Hackensack station with them. She called me to come right over."

A cold breeze that had nothing to do with the open windows swept through me.

"When was this?"

"About an hour ago."

"What did the cops look like?"

"One was tall and thin, kind of nice looking in an outdoorsy kind of way. Looked like he could use a good meal, though. Or a new suit. The other one was—"

I hardly heard the rest and hung up as soon as I could. Damn Brodsky! Bad enough he's constantly on my case, but when he starts harassing my friends, it's time I let him know I've had enough.

Fifteen minutes later I pulled into the parking lot of the Bergen County prosecutor's office.

Alighting from my car, I was just in time to see Meg get into hers. I yelled at her to wait, but she seemed not to hear me and drove off. I stood there indecisively, not sure if I should stick with my original plan or follow her. I went with my first impulse. I could catch up with Meg later. I wanted to have it out with Brodsky while I still had the nerve.

I marched into the office feeling belligerent as hell, ready to barrel past anyone who tried to stop me. But Brodsky's name was an open sesame, and I was waved on without comment. Several detectives were sitting around the congested squad room, scribbling at their desks, talking on phones. I spotted Brodsky next to a water cooler, paper cup in hand. I was tempted to grab it and dump it over his head, but I held my temper and planted myself firmly between him and the cooler.

"Lieutenant."

He didn't seem surprised to see me. Very deliberately he finished drinking, then reached around me and tossed the cup into the wastebasket.

"Something I can do for you?"

"You brought my friend, Meg Reilly, here for questioning!"

"Yeah," he said, unperturbed. "Right."

"You've got to stop this. It's one thing, your badgering me incessantly with your questions. Like it or not, I'm involved in this mess. But it's really lousy and—and unethical—to drag my friends into it."

"Maybe you should choose your friends more carefully."

"What?" I hadn't expected that.

"Maybe," he replied with exaggerated patience, "you should—"

"I heard you. What the hell is that supposed to mean?"

He took my arm and led me over to his desk.

"Sit," he said.

"I'd rather stand."

He shrugged. "Whatever."

He sat, and I stood, feeling something of a fool, like the king in *The King and I*, who didn't allow anyone's head to be higher than his.

Brodsky drummed his fingers on the metal desk. "Your friend's a real looker, isn't she."

I was so shocked, I sat down. What was this? It didn't jibe with my impression of him.

"Tell me something I don't know," I said stiffly.

"Okay. Did you know she knew your husband?"

"Well, of course she knows him. She's been at the house when he comes to—"

"I mean, before you and she met."

. . . *before you met, before you met* ricocheted off the wall, took a few seconds to penetrate. My first instinct was to deny and defend.

"For your information, Meg only moved here from the city after Rich and I were separated, so—"

"She did some modeling for him several years back."

When I was ten years old, I was kicked by a horse. It felt exactly the same way. A minute went by before I dredged up enough breath to speak.

"That's not true!" But the worm of suspicion lying dormant in my gut reared its head.

"Her picture was in that pile you found yesterday," he said quietly. "That's why I brought her in."

"Why are you telling me these lies?" I wanted to cry. But then I remembered Meg reaching for the pictures, her face gone suddenly pale, and all I managed was a whispered, "I don't believe you," while I twisted the braided strap on my handbag into an irretrievable knot.

He reached into a folder and pulled out a photograph. I could see where it had been taped together. He slid it across the desk to me.

The face in the photo was Meg—Meg a few years younger, made up more glamorously than I'd ever seen her. I saw something in Brodsky's eyes then, like he cared that I had to see this, that he had to tell me these things, like you see in the eyes of a friend. But I know better than to believe what I see in someone's eyes. Friends betray. I was becoming an expert on betrayal.

"Carrie, she admitted it."

"What?" I whispered.

"She used to be a professional photographer. Your husband saw some of her work and hired her for a shoot, then offered her a job modeling. Ms. Reilly had two photo sessions using various products," he continued, his tone flat. "The picture here was for eye makeup. When she showed up for a body cream shoot, she discovered there was no photographer, and your husband wanted her to model nude while he applied the cream and shot the pictures himself."

This was another of my nightmares.

"None of Rich's ads use nude models," I protested nonsensically.

"The photos were obviously not for public display."

That was pity in his voice. I didn't want his pity. I wanted him to be lying. They say troubles come in threes. So this had to be the end of it. After today nothing bad could happen to me. My children and I could live happily ever after.

Brodsky had the sensitivity to keep his eyes averted. "For whatever it's worth, she says she turned the job down."

She says. "Why didn't Meg tell me she knew Rich?"

"You'll have to ask her."

"Was . . . did she ever see him again? I mean until she met me?"

"She says she didn't."

It came back to me then, Meg's knowing what I'd said to Rich that night. How could she have known that unless Rich had told her?

"Do you know anything about her past, Carrie?"

"Not . . . much." I sounded funny, like I had a bad cold. "She never talks about herself. Only that she was married, and her husband died."

"Her husband isn't dead. He's in the federal pen in Danbury."

One lie after the other. Like Rich.

"She goes . . . that must be where she goes every week when . . . she must go up to Connecticut to visit him."

"Sounds right."

"What'd he—what's he in for?"

Brodsky made a big thing of straightening out the papers in the file and closing it.

"Conspiracy to cover up a fraud. Your friend was an unindicted co-conspirator."

How do you get to be an unindicted co-conspirator? I thought. *What is an unindicted co-conspirator anyway? If you're a co-conspirator, why don't they indict you?*

It was all too much for my overloaded brain. I went numb. I think there's only so much shock the human mind can absorb at one time. After that there's a protective mechanism that kicks in and you stop feeling. At least it seems to work that way with me. But I must have been shaking because Brodsky came around the desk and put his jacket over my shoulders. I'm not sure if it was the jacket or his hands on my shoulders, but after a minute, sensation returned.

I got unsteadily to my feet and handed the coat back to him. "I have to go. I have patients coming."

"I'll have someone drive you."

"I have my car." Politely, I held out my hand. "Well, good-bye, Lieutenant. Thanks for the information."

"I'll walk you out."

He guided me to the door. I concentrated on putting one foot in front of the other and managed to get down the steps without falling. He led me around to the passenger side.

"Give me your keys."

"I can drive."

"You can't walk. Give me your keys."

Robotlike, I handed them over. I was hardly aware of getting into the car or of him getting behind the wheel and starting the engine. But I was aware that he reached out and covered my hand with his.

IT'S AN INTERESTING phenomenon that, when you have children, there's some kind of inner strength that takes over and keeps you going. I had to earn a living. There was no way I was going to keep my practice if I kept canceling appointments.

So I saw all my clients. From somewhere outside myself I watched as I weighed my overeaters and moderated their discussion on addictive behavior. I even remained detached when Melanie Greenwald brought up the murders right in the middle of a group exercise on the destructiveness of displaced anger.

"Maybe they should be looking for a fatty," she said.

"Excuse me?"

"You know. The person who knocked off your husband's sweetie pie and his secretary. The cops should be looking for an overeater."

So much for my hope that they might not connect me with the case.

"Why do you say that?" I asked in a well-modulated tone while the group gave a concerted gasp at her temerity.

"Whoever did it's mad as hell—I mean angry-mad, not nuts. But like you're always telling us, he or she needs to direct the anger where it belongs!"

Thank God I weigh in at a hundred and ten pounds.

Ruth-Ann's face turned blotchy. "Why don't you just shut up, Melanie!"

A shocked silence settled over the group. No one but me had ever seen Ruth-Ann angry. Everybody looked at her, then at me, then self-consciously looked away.

"It's an interesting theory, Melanie," I said, shooting Ruth-Ann a reassuring "I can handle this" look. "I'll be sure to mention it to the police."

Somehow I got through the rest of the session and saw three more patients without dissolving into hysterics.

Mr. Tobin came at six. He's a tall thin man in his sixties, with round glasses and sparse gray hair, who walks kind of bent to one side like a poplar in a windstorm. I have a feeling that before his wife died last December, he walked straighter. When he came to me, his blood pressure was one-ninety over one-ten. By watching the biofeedback monitor, he's learning how his thoughts and emotions adversely affect his body. I'm teaching him techniques to regain control.

I like Mr. Tobin. I like how he misses his wife, how he talks about her with such tenderness in his voice. Widows and widowers tend to idealize their dead spouses. You'd think they'd all been married to saints. But I believe Mr. Tobin. Even dead, I envy Mrs. Tobin.

At seven I had Jerry Grinch—my "grinch who stole Christmas," which I am certain he is capable of doing. Jerry is seventeen. His hair is cut in a mohawk that stands straight up on his head and is dyed green. He wears lots of black leather, high studded cowboy boots, and a hanging rhinestone earring in his left ear. I don't think he's into anything stronger than marijuana, but it's not doing much for his powers of concentration. I'm trying, without much success, to convince him that he can achieve a satisfactory high from brain-wave training, without drug-related memory loss. Jerry's father is president of a bank in Greenwich, Connecticut, and his mother is a fund-raiser for some historical society. They bring him to Piermont for therapy in the hope they won't run into anyone they know.

We went through our usual bit.

"Take off the earring, Jerry," I instructed, as I do at every session.

"Aw, shit," he replied, as he does at every session.

"If I get a good reading first time around, I won't have to pinch your ears."

"Yeah, yeah, yeah."

I always have a tough time getting a correct reading on the impedance meter when I do Jerry. After I've applied gel and attached the sensors to his head and earlobes, I plug the cable into the meter. A low reading means I have a good contact. With Jerry, I usually have to reapply the gel two or three times, rub the spot on his head extra hard where the sensor is attached, and pinch his ears with the earclips. I think the problem is the green hair dye.

"Ow," he yelled, as I pinched.

"Sorry," I said.

Halfway through the session he'd had enough of the blinking lights on the monitor. "Hey, I'm gettin' sick of red and green. How about throwin' in some oranges and purples?"

"We're not shooting for psychedelic, Jerry."

"Who needs it?" he muttered sulkily and turned off, turning all the lights red. No amount of discussion could entice him to focus, so I removed the sensors and sent him out to the reception area to wait for his mother, with a note to have her call me.

Jerry and Vickie back to back are enough to send me shrieking to Meg's Place for my chamomile fix.

Not tonight, though. I didn't want to see Meg tonight.

Vickie came promptly at eight, looking like Isadora Duncan, all legs and flowing chiffon. I forced myself to concentrate on preparing her for the interview. We spent part of the session working on relaxation exercises. Then

I hooked her up to the EEG computer for some alpha-theta training, while I gave her positive affirmations to build self-confidence. Alpha-theta is the dreamy meditative brain state in which the person training becomes somewhat suggestible. Vickie closed her eyes, and while she listened to the beeps from the software and the soft music in the background, I began talking.

"While you're relaxing, Vickie, say to yourself, 'I feel confident. I'm intelligent, attractive, clever, and determined. I can accomplish whatever I set out to do. I'm in control of my life. I can make good things happen to me. I can overcome any obstacle and defeat any problem. I am a winner, and I am taking charge of my life.'" I stopped as I saw Vickie smile and mouth the words *"I am a winner, I'm taking charge of my life."* I allowed her to sit there for fifteen minutes repeating the positive "self-talk" over and over. Then I took off the sensors, and, for the final few minutes, guided her into a visualization of herself dressed in a smart black suit, wowing the powers that be with her expertise. When we finished, she hugged me. It was one of those experiences that make me feel really good about what I do.

I didn't check my phone messages till I was ready to leave. When I did, I wished I hadn't. There were two messages from television reporters and one from the *Phoenix* reporter, all wanting to know if I knew where Rich was, asking me to get back to them before talking to anyone else, and hinting at vague rewards if I would be cooperative. It had gotten out that I was the one who found Dot's body, and the vultures had begun to smell a sensational story.

There were also two hang-ups and a terse message from Meg.

"Carrie, please stop by after work. The chamomile's brewing."

What was she trying to pull?

It was dark when I locked up and crept out of the building. My cloak of numbness had dissipated. I no longer felt anesthetized, and as I walked to my car, I kept looking over my shoulder, expecting a TV crew or a killer—I wasn't sure which would be worse—to come crashing through the bushes. Every footstep, every shadow, caused heart palpitations. As I passed Meg's Place, I saw her standing behind the counter, laughing with her customers. I started to run, putting distance between us.

Bits and pieces tumbled around in my head, jogged loose by my pounding feet. Rich . . . Meg . . . Brodsky's hand on mine, making me shiver when I wasn't cold. Where was Rich, anyway? And Meg. My *friend* Meg, who had turned out to be as great a liar and cheat as my husband. My fury grew as I remembered the names she'd invented for him.

"Lock up your daughters, your wives, your goats," she'd giggle when Rich came to pick up the kids. "Here comes Dick the Prick," or "Mighty Louse," or her favorite, "Superphallus." She, who probably knew as well as I, the size and shape of that organ! How could she have looked me in the eye!

Why hadn't I asked Brodsky when I had the chance

what the fraud was that Meg's husband had been convicted of, and what Meg's part in it had been? I'd been so stunned, my brain had shut down. But now it made sense, her knowing criminal lawyers. And the logical conclusion—if Meg had lied about her past and about knowing Rich, what else had she lied about? And why?

I arrived breathless at my car and fumbled with the lock. A throbbing pain began in my temples and spread over my eyes. *Stop!* I told myself as I tried to breathe it away. But the pain and the thoughts that were causing it wouldn't let up. What could Erica or Dot possibly have had on Meg? Nude photos, maybe? Not worth killing over. Meg didn't have the kind of career or relationship with a man that could be affected by that type of exposure. What, then? Was there some sinister connection between Meg and Rich? Had Erica and Dot known something so terrible, they'd been murdered for it? Could blackmail have been the motive? In spite of what I'd told Brodsky about Rich being nonviolent, I was having second thoughts. Rich is a coward, and like most cowards he can be a bully. A cornered bully is a dangerous animal.

I got in the car and pressed the button that locked all the doors.

Maybe they'd known something that could incriminate Meg in her husband's illegal activities. Maybe Rich had been trying to protect her. Against his own fiancée? Improbable. Maybe he'd been involved in something with her and her husband. *But Rich isn't a killer,* my mind kept insisting. After living with him for eighteen years, I'd know that about him . . . wouldn't I?

Something that had happened months before Rich left came back to me.

He'd come home late. Nothing unusual, at that particular juncture in our marriage. I'd quit hassling him about it.

I was already in bed, absorbed in the newest Sara Paretsky. The cats were curled up against me. Horton lay at my feet, gnawing happily on a rawhide chew stick. When he heard Rich's footsteps, he slunk off the bed and retreated to a safe position behind the TV set.

Rich was in a bad mood. "Get those stinking cats off the bed!" was his affectionate greeting as he grabbed a handful of comforter and shook it. Lucie and Placido streaked off the bed and out of the room. José stood his ground—or rather, his bed—and spit.

"Don't you dare!" I grabbed the cat just before Rich's hand came down. "Don't you ever hit one of my animals!"

"I've told you, I don't want them on the bed," he snarled. "God-damned cats're more important to you than I am."

"It's not a competition," I shot back, provoked into equal nastiness. I stroked José's ruffled coat and put him outside the room. Horton followed, tail between his legs. I shut the door, determined to make peace.

"What's the matter, Rich? The cats never used to bother you. What's going on?"

I thought he wasn't going to answer. He pulled on his pajama bottoms, unbuttoned his shirt, tossed it onto the chair. "Lot on my mind."

"Can't you tell me?"

He crawled into bed then and laid his head on my breast. I stroked his hair, grateful for the rare moment of intimacy.

"Problem at the plant. I'll handle it."

"What kind of problem?"

"Formula stolen. Industrial sabotage. Happens all the time. Never happened to me before, though."

"Who?" I asked, horrified. "It'd have to be somebody on the inside."

I could feel the heat of his anger through his scalp and his voice sounded raspy, almost unrecognizable.

"Don't know. But I'll find out. And when I do, you can bet your life the bastard won't be in a condition to ever do it again!"

At the time it sounded like an idle threat, the kind we all make at one time or another. And I never heard the end of the story, although on several occasions I'd asked. If Rich ever found out who had sabotaged him, he never told me about it.

Recalling his words now, though, I felt chilled. Was it possible Rich could be involved in these horrible killings? And Meg—was I seriously considering that Meg and Rich were in some sort of conspiracy? Meg, who had been a loving, loyal friend, there for me through the worst crisis in my life. How could I believe she could be involved in something so hideous as murder?

Against my will answers came to me. Meg had lied on more than one occasion. She'd tried to stop me from searching Dot's apartment. And when I'd insisted, she'd stayed downstairs with the doorman, making sure I went up to the apartment alone.

ALLIE WAS DOWNSTAIRS waiting for me when I walked in. She didn't give me my customary peck on the cheek. Horton did, though. Standing on his hind legs, he planted slurpy kisses over my entire face. It was a measure of my sense of abandonment that I was grateful for them.

"Why didn't you tell us?" Allie's tone was accusatory.

"What didn't I tell you?"

"About Dot."

I was at a loss. "What's the matter with you? Meg told you."

"She didn't tell us you were the one who found her!"

"Well, I guess she didn't think—" I stopped, helpless in the face of her anger.

"Everybody in school was asking us about it. We felt like geeks!"

Meg had said she hadn't told the kids the worst of it, but why hadn't she told them my finding the body was the reason I was so upset? Was she trying to shield them, or was there another reason? I was too weary to figure it out. I put my briefcase on the coffee table and sank down on the couch. Placido crawled onto my lap and revved up his motor.

"I'm sorry. I thought she had."

"How come you went to Dot's, anyway? You couldn't stand her."

I lied to my daughter. "I thought maybe Dad might be there." Just what I needed. The third degree in my own living room. She might as well have been Brodsky. "Where's Matt?"

"Upstairs."

"What's with him tonight? He's usually howling for a second dinner when I get home this late."

No reply.

I dumped Placido onto the floor and got to my feet. The cat stalked away in a manner that would have done his namesake proud. I went to the bar, poured myself a glass of wine, and took a big gulp. "Allie?"

"He got in a fight," she muttered.

I choked on the wine. "A fight? Matt?" My Mattie's the least pugnacious ten-year-old male I've ever met. He's a natural-born mediator. "Is he okay?"

"Yeah, Mrs. Randolph broke it up."

"What was it over?"

"I don't know. I—I think somebody said something . . ."

"About what?" I dreaded the answer. "About what, Allie?"

She squirmed. "Doesn't matter. The kid he was fighting with's a dork."

"It matters to me. What was the fight over?"

From the foot of the stairs came Matt's high childish voice. "He said you did it. 'Cause you were the only one had a motive."

I lost the ability to speak or move.

"You didn't go it, did you, Mom?" Matt's voice cracked as he spoke, but I heard him loud and clear.

The glass fell from my fingers and shattered on the edge of the bar. I stared at my child who, because of me, had two nasty red bruises just beginning to swell on his cheek and who was asking me this outrageous question. "Matt," I gasped. "Oh, Mattie . . . no!"

He looked at me, then looked at his feet. Allie's eyes darted from one to the other of us. She started to cry.

"Sorry," Matt mumbled finally, "I didn't mean—" But as I reached out for him, he backed away. "Where's Dad? I want Dad to be here!"

I couldn't take any more. I made a dash for the stairs. When I got to my room, I locked the door and leaned against it, so totally bereft, I couldn't stop shivering. I think—and this includes the day Rich left—I think seeing the look of doubt and shame in Matt's eyes was the very lowest point of my entire life.

I heard the doorbell ring, but I didn't have the strength or the will to change position.

"Who is it?" I heard Allie call out.

"It's Meg, Allie. I want to talk to your mom."

I wished I were a witch like the Elizabeth Montgomery character in that old sitcom, so I could wiggle my nose and send her to Mars. I opened my door a crack. Horton pushed past it and lay with his nose on my feet.

"I don't want to see anyone, Allie," I called in a stage whisper.

Shocked silence. Then: "But Mom, it's Meg."

"I know who it is. Tell her to go away!" And I sank down on the floor and buried my face in Horton's wriggling comforting body.

Somehow we all got to bed. I hope the children slept. I didn't.

F R I D A Y
MAY 28

BREAKFAST WAS A SILENT
ordeal. I saw the anxiety and confusion etched on those two small faces, but there was nothing I could do to erase it. Fortunately, they both had weekend plans, so I hugged them hard, told them to have fun, smiled, and waved as the car pool pulled away. Then I wandered into the living room and sat at my desk. Life went on, bills had to be

paid. I wrote checks for the mortgage and the electricity bill, then sorted through the rest, deciding which could be postponed. My eyes fell on Arthur's bill, and I grimaced as I wrote a check for two hundred dollars, appending a note that I thought Mirimar's charges were an outrage, that it was his job to call them to task, but that I would agree to part of it if I could pay it off in installments.

Mirimar. Meg and I had never followed through on that. Events had intervened, and I'd forgotten about our plan. Now, whatever investigating was going to get done, was going to get done by me alone.

I glanced at my watch, then back to Mirimar's itemized bill. Their office was in Fort Lee, about half an hour's drive. The investigator's initials were P.R.

If I rushed, I could get to their office by nine, talk to this guy, and be at my office for my eleven o'clock. Maybe I could find out what kind of car had been cruising in front of the house that day, maybe I could trace the killer.

When I was combing my hair, the phone rang, but I let the machine get it.

"Carrie, you can't avoid me forever. Please pick up if you're there." Meg's voice, disturbed, pained. I remembered her performance with the doorman, tears arriving on cue. Boy, had she missed her calling! What an actress! I didn't answer.

A sigh, then angrily: "Okay, you don't want to hear my explanation? You want to sulk and lick your wounds? Fine!

I'm here whenever you decide to behave like an adult!" The phone clicked off.

"Go buy some Band-Aids, *pal*," I said out loud, grabbing my bag. "You're going to have a few wounds of your own to lick before I'm through!"

I'd barely locked the front door when I heard a car pull up. As if conjured from my subconscious, there stood Ted Brodsky.

"I have an appointment, Lieutenant," I said, trying my best to appear unruffled.

"You on the way to your office?"

"Not till eleven. But—"

"I need a few minutes."

What now? "Why?"

"We need to talk."

He seemed much cooler than he had last night.

"Last time we talked, jumping off the G.W. bridge seemed a viable option."

"I was only the messenger."

"Yeah, well, they kill messengers—" I stopped. Why did everything I said seem to have something to do with murder?

"You don't have to watch every word," he said, his tone friendly.

I was confused. About his change of manner and about my reaction to him. I studied his face. So impassive, so controlled. Impossible to tell what he was thinking.

He hadn't seemed like an adversary yesterday. The effect of his touch on me aside, the guy hadn't been making a pass. He'd been showing compassion, one human being to another. And the way his clothes hung on him sort of touched me, as if he didn't care how he looked because he had nobody who cared about him. But he was the law. Anything I said might be used against me. Maybe this sudden friendliness was an act, part of some plan to get me to incriminate myself.

He glanced at me impatiently. "Shall we go inside?"

I hesitated, debating whether to tell him about Mirimar. Last night I'd sworn never to trust anyone, and here I was, wanting to share information with this cop.

Well, I wasn't a criminal. And what the Mirimar investigator had to say might help to find the killer. Which would clear me. So I told him about the bill, and Sue Tomkins seeing the car, and my deduction that this investigator might have gotten a make on the vehicle.

"That's where I was going now," I concluded.

"Why didn't you tell me about this before?"

"I'm telling you now."

"Get in. I'll go with you."

I got in.

We were silent for the next couple of blocks. I stared straight ahead, very aware of him, annoyed with myself for being aware. At the light he looked over at me. "You okay?"

"Aside from the fact that I'm involved in two murders, my best friend's betrayed me, my husband's left me and taken off for parts unknown, and my son doubts me, I'm terrific."

His smile accentuated the little wrinkles around his eyes. "What's this about your son?"

"Somebody in school said I was the only one with a motive. He got in a fight over it."

"Sounds to me like a kid who loves his mother."

I swallowed, then got the words out. "He asked me if I did it."

"So he wanted a little reassurance. Hey, the kid took a black eye for you."

"Bruised cheeks."

His fingers brushed the smudges under my eyes, and my disobedient heart skipped a beat.

"You look like you've been in a fight yourself."

"I didn't sleep very well."

Conversation lagged as we turned onto the parkway. The trees were in full bloom, splashes of green and white and pink on either side of the road. Normally I love this time of year. This year my spirit had lost its wings.

"You know," I murmured, making an effort to break the silence, "you've probably found out everything there is to know about me, but I don't know a thing about you other than your profession."

"Not much to know."

"You have children?"

"Never married." He held up a hand. "Don't say it. I know what you mental health people think about that."

"I'm a little soured on marriage myself right now. Anyway, I guessed you weren't married. If you were, you'd have a jacket that fit."

"It used to fit," he said. "It will again in about a month."

"You've been sick?"

"Spent a little time in the hospital. Food was lousy."

"What was the matter?"

He paused briefly. "A little run-in with a shooter."

I jumped. "You were shot!?"

"Nothing life-threatening."

But his words had jolted me.

There's a technique we teach in biofeedback. When you find yourself in a situation that activates your "fight or flight" response and the adrenaline is flowing, you stop and ask yourself, "Is this a life-threatening situation?" If it isn't, and most aren't, you employ relaxation techniques, assuring yourself that you can cope, thus reserving that adrenaline flow for the rarer moments when you might meet Tyrannosaurus rex. In that instance you assess the situation, then choose between standing your ground or running like hell.

I assessed my situation. Ted Brodsky was in a life-threatening business. What was I doing getting ideas about this guy? He was a detective conducting a murder investigation, and I, much as I wanted to deny it, was a suspect. I was most definitely in a life-threatening situation. If he wasn't Tyrannosaurus, he was about as close to one as I ever want to get.

We turned off Lemoine Avenue onto Center Street.

"I think it's that red brick building on the corner," I said, keeping my voice businesslike. "This is number 421, so that must be 425."

He pulled into the lot, cut the motor, and turned to look at me. He knew exactly what I'd been thinking. There was amusement in his eyes, and something I couldn't quite read. Disappointment?

I fumbled around for the door handle, couldn't find it. His rough jacket brushed my arm as he reached across and opened it.

"If I'm calling you Carrie," he said, his mouth too close to my ear, "I guess it's only fair you start calling me Ted."

"Okay," I replied breathlessly, as every hair on my head began to tingle. "Fair is fair." And I flew out of the car and ran like hell to the safety of the impersonal lobby.

MIRIMAR SECURITY WAS located on the first floor in the last office on the left, at the rear of the building. I beat Brodsky to the door by at least ten strides. I needed time to deal with my reaction, which, I assured myself, was clearly the result of a crisis-triggered vulnerability. Classic hostage, like Patty Hearst who, having lost control of her life, related romantically to her kidnapper. I would eventually come to my senses.

The reception area was small, sparsely furnished with a truncated green vinyl couch, a walnut lamp table scratched in more places than my son's dirt bike, and a straight-back wooden armchair. The swimsuit edition of *Sports Illustrated* was the only reading material in sight.

A dour gray-haired woman, wearing almost no makeup, a grouchy expression, and a lavender pantsuit with a polka-dotted blouse, sat behind a glass partition filing her nails. She slid back the window without missing a stroke.

"Yes?"

"I'm looking for one of your investigators," I began,

ignoring the gentle nudge in my back. "I don't know his name, but his initials are P.R."

"What is it in reference to?"

"I'm Caroline Carlin Burnham. Your firm was hired by my lawyer, Arthur Carboni, to look into my husband's— uh—business affairs. I've seen the investigator's report, and I'd like to talk with him."

Her expression metamorphosed from grouchy to suspicious. She dropped the emery board, swiveled her chair ninety degrees, and mumbled a few inaudible words into the intercom. Then she swiveled back. "I'm sorry. Mr. Rostow is out on a case."

"Well then, I'd like to speak with someone else in charge."

The pressure between my shoulder blades accelerated to painful, and I felt myself nudged away from the window. A flash of the badge later, and we were ushered into an office approximately the size of my linen closet and seated across from Peter Rostow himself, who miraculously had managed, unobserved by us, to slip his massive body into his office.

Rostow was a fiftyish guy with the florid complexion of an alcoholic and an off-center flattened nose on his truly ugly face. It turned out there were three partners in Mirimar, Rostow being one of them, all of whom worked in the field. Aside from Madame Polka-dot, there were no other employees.

Rostow was wary at first, fearful we'd come to challenge his time sheets. When he realized we were here for information not directly related to my case, he relaxed, his smile revealing a missing tooth on the lower right side of his jaw, which I conjectured had been knocked out by an irate client.

"Always happy to assist the police," he simpered, ignoring me and turning to Brodsky.

Brodsky finished flipping through the report Rostow had handed him. "Did you see anything at all suspicious on any of the days you watched Mr. Burnham's home?"

"Nothing unusual. All in the report."

"Did Ms. Vogel ever have visitors to the house when Mr. Burnham wasn't there?"

"It'd be in the report."

"Specifically male visitors."

Rostow picked up the sheaf of papers and flipped a few pages. "March tenth, mailman came at one thirty-five, Saturday the seventeenth, he, Burnham was home, no visitors. She went out at two-fifteen, he left shortly after, I followed him, he went to Englewood for a haircut, place on Dean Drive called—"

"Maybe you noticed something that didn't seem important to my case, so you didn't make a note of it," I interrupted, ignoring the pressure of Brodsky's foot on my little toe.

"Listen, it was more'n a month ago. If I didn't put it in the report, I'm not gonna remember now."

"Try. I mean, like maybe a car stopped at another house and nobody got out, or maybe the same one was cruising the street on all the days you—"

"Mrs. Burnham." Rostow's tone was patronizing, the tone of a man who assumes all women are either premenstrual or menopausal, incapable of logic. "We're a reputable agency. I staked out your husband's place on three separate occasions. I reported everything relevant to the case." He leafed through the typewritten report. "One, that Mr. Burnham was livin' with a Ms. Erica Vogel, not his wife, two that—"

"That's what was irrelevant," I snapped. "I knew he was living with her. He left me to live with her. I don't give a damn what was in his garbage bin. Why the hell were you wasting your time and my money on stuff like that?"

The pain in my foot shut my mouth.

"Let's stick to the subject," Brodsky said calmly. "I'm interested in the woman he met at this restaurant in the Village—Haji's, you say here. What'd she look like?"

Rostow threw a malignant look in my direction. *"Very* attractive. Tall, thin."

"How old, approximately?"

"Hard to say. Couldn't see her face that well. She had on sunglasses."

"What color hair?"

"Couldn't tell. She had some kinda beret thing on her head."

"Couldn't see her face, couldn't see her hair, but you could tell she was attractive," I muttered.

"So her hair was either short or tucked into the hat," Ted continued, shooting me a "shut your mouth or I'll get the other foot" glance. "What was she wearing?"

"A raincoat. Long, to her ankles."

"How long did they stay?"

Rostow screwed up his face, trying to recall details. It

made him look like a Cabbage Patch doll. "Think they only had one drink. She got mad. Threw a bunch of pretzels at him and ran out."

Didn't sound like a business lunch to me. So Rich had probably been cheating on Erica. Herb Golinko was right. One woman, no matter who she was, wasn't ever going to be enough for Rich. I wondered why Brodsky was pursuing it. Did he think there was a conspiracy? Then Meg's face popped into my mind. Meg is tall and slim.

"Mr. Rostow," Brodsky continued. "you say here that you interviewed employees at Mr. Burnham's company in an effort to determine—what?"

"Guys hide money in divorce actions," he said belligerently. "Wanna keep as much as they can get away with. Lots of times, somebody in the office lets somethin' slip. I was doin' my job."

"I'm sure you were," Brodsky replied. "Did you come up with anything?"

"It'd be in the report."

I tucked my feet safely under the chair. "You were padding your bill!"

Rostow shot to his feet. "I got nothin' more to say to you, lady!"

In a flash I was on my feet, confronting him, nose to nose. "Yeah? Well, how'd you like to come down to the precinct?"

Off to my right, I heard what sounded like a death rattle. I glanced at Brodsky. He looked like a man about to strangle someone. I assumed if I kept this up, that would be me. I sat back down.

For some reason, maybe it was Brodsky's expression, Rostow's manner suddenly altered. "Wait a minute," he said. "Maybe I do remember somethin' else."

"Is it in the report?" I inquired sweetly.

"No, it ain't in the report 'cause it didn't have nothin' to do with your divorce, though I sure can see why *your* husband wanted out!"

I was about to come back with a vaporizing retort when Brodsky tromped so hard on my foot, he cut off my breath.

"Sit down, Mr. Rostow."

Brodsky's voice was level, but the authority it carried brooked no contradiction. Rostow sat.

"Go on."

"I had a chat with the secretary."

I caught my breath.

"Dorothy Shea?" Brodsky asked, his face impassive.

"Yeah, one I read got whacked."

Brodsky said nothing. Between the pain in my foot and the knot in my gut, I couldn't have said anything.

"She was really down on this Vogel dame. You'd've thought she was the wife. Said, and I quote, she knew thing's'd get the slut fired."

"What kinds of things?" Brodsky asked.

"Somethin' about kickbacks."

Perspiration trickled down my neck. I found my voice. "If she knew something like that, why wouldn't she have told Rich? Maybe she was inventing it."

"Don't think so. Took her to a bar, and she'd had a

couple. Loosened her tongue. Told me more'n she probably meant to."

I was shocked. "Did she know who you were?"

"Mrs. Burnham, I'm not stupid."

Me either, so I let that one go.

Brodsky tapped his pencil impatiently. "Okay, Vogel was taking kickbacks? How? In cash?"

"Shea said she didn't have absolute proof, so she couldn't tell her boss. Said she was bidin' her time."

"Who were the kickbacks coming from?"

"Well, Vogel was in the marketing department, so—"

I grabbed Brodsky's arm. "She was head of marketing. Everything had to go through her office."

Rostow nodded. "Yeah, well, I guess she was in a position to throw business in certain directions. Only thing the Shea dame said she knew for a fact was that Vogel was spendin' a lot of time and money at Elizabeth Arden's in the city, and she was pretty damned sure it was courtesy of the Wallace-Bowden ad agency."

I T WAS PAST ten when we finished with Rostow and left the building.

"I'm crippled," I grumbled. "Couldn't you've—?"

"Christ, Carrie, what bad movie'd you get that 'come down to the precinct' crap from?"

"No movie. From you."

"What? I never—"

"Yes, you did. Walking down to the pier on Monday.

You were trying to scare me. And it worked, so I thought I'd give it a shot."

He started to laugh.

"Why do you suppose she'd do something like that? Erica, I mean."

"Greed." He offered his arm. "Grab hold."

I did, enjoying the contact, and hobbled along, trying to match his long strides. "But she had a good job. And they were going to be married right after the divorce."

"Remember, he was insisting she sign a prenuptial. It meant your children came first. Maybe she was getting even."

That sounded like Erica.

"You were asking him about men," I said as we arrived at the car. "Who told you Erica was cheating on Rich?"

"Dot Shea."

"Well, I guess turnabout is fair play. He was cheating on her."

"We don't know that. We don't know who the woman in the restaurant was."

Herb Golinko knew about Rich's women, though. And Dot would probably have known. She took all his calls, opened his mail, knew how many times a day he went to the bathroom. But how would she have known about Erica's activities? "Did she say who Erica was fooling around with?"

"Client. Maybe there's a connection with the ad agency. I'll check it out."

"Blackmail," I muttered. I scrambled into the car and pressed the button to unlock Ted's side. "Who might've been blackmailing Erica?" Meg came to mind. Maybe that was what the fight in Haji's was about. Except I couldn't see Meg throwing pretzels. She'd be more likely to have thrown a bottle.

"Why kill her? Nothing to gain with her dead."

"Okay, okay, lemme think." There had to be a way these unconnected bits of information fit together. "Maybe Dot was blackmailing Erica, they had a fight—no, that wouldn't make sense. Because then who killed Dot?"

"Maybe your husband found out about the affair or the kickbacks or both, and *they* had a fight. And then maybe he realized Dot Shea could have incriminated him."

"She wouldn't have." Dot's instinct to protect and defend Rich was as ingrained as mine had always been. "I can't believe that Rich's capable of . . ."

"Madame Therapist," Brodsky said, not unkindly. "When are you going to face up to who Rich Burnham is?"

"I know who he is," I replied uncomfortably. "I've learned a lot this past year. I know he's weak and he uses people."

"He's worse. He's a liar, a cheat, and a fraud."

Why did that keep hurting? "But not a killer." I didn't want my children's father to be a killer.

"Not under ordinary circumstances, but maybe when push came to shove—"

I shook my head adamantly. "You don't live with a man for eighteen years and not know something like that."

Was I trying to convince myself or Brodsky?

He actually groaned. "Christ, Carrie, I've heard that so many times, it's gotten to be a joke. 'John? I've known him for years. Wonderful guy, wouldn't swat a mosquito.' And I'm there when they find his baby with a pillow over its head because it wouldn't stop crying." He was silent for a minute. Then he said softly. "You'd think you'd get used to it. You never do."

We were on the parkway. My mind drifted back to another spring when I was in the car on the Palisades Parkway.

I was ready to give birth to Allie. We were racing into the city to New York University Hospital. I remember Rich's reassuring voice when I panicked because the contractions were coming faster and harder than I had been led to believe in our Lamaze classes, and I was losing control of the breathing exercises. I remember his soothing hand rubbing my back, the gentle way he calmed my fears, got me back on track. I remember his sitting by my bed all night when things went wrong, and I had to have an emergency cesarean. And I remember his railing at the nurse who was late with my pain medication. Was this a man who could murder the woman he loved?

On the heels of that recollection came the memory of the morning Matt was born, a mere two years later. I saw Rich standing in the doorway of the operating room having refused my request to come in, ignoring me as he discussed his latest investment with my obstetrician. And I remember his leaving for the office as soon as Matt was delivered. Still, that only meant there had been a change in his feelings for me, a change that the birth of a son had, for a time, obscured. It didn't make him capable of murder.

Ted and I said little until we arrived at my office.

"I haven't got my car," I murmured as I stood on the curb. "I should've had you drop me at home."

"I'll pick you up," he replied. "What time do you finish?"

Suddenly I just wanted to be alone. "Six. But don't bother. I have to do some shopping. I'll grab a cab."

Again I had the feeling he'd read my mind.

"Right." His voice was cool. "See you."

THE FIRST MESSAGE on my answering machine was Ruth-Ann reminding me that Monday was Memorial Day and asking if we were still having overeaters group. Would I please call her and let her know? The second was Vickie wanting to tell me all about the interview. She'd call me back later at home. I put my head down on my desk and listened to Hamilton Grinch blast me because Jerry was refusing to come for training, did I know why? Yeah, I knew why. He was given everything he wanted, including enough money to buy recreational drugs. He had no reason to make the effort to change.

When a familiar voice said, "Carrie?" I thought it was coming from the machine. No message followed, and I looked up. Rich was leaning against the doorframe, his left arm in a sling, his drawn face a patchwork of Band-Aids.

Strangely, I felt none of the old preprogrammed emotions—not shock, not concern at his appearance—only a mild curiosity as to the cause of the injuries, and anger for Matt and Allie's sakes.

"Where the hell've you been?"

"Lay off, will you?" He held up his hand as if warding off a blow, limped over to the leather recliner, and dropped into it. "I was in a car wreck."

He waited for my response—a word of sympathy for his suffering, or at the very least relief that he was okay. I couldn't manage it.

"Whose car? Yours is in your lot."

"A friend's. What's the matter? Don't you believe me?"

"The police've been looking for you. They checked the hospitals."

"I didn't go to a hospital."

"Who set your arm?"

"A doctor. Someone this friend sent me to."

Lady or man, I wanted to ask. "What friend?"

"What's the difference?"

Half a story. Why couldn't he ever tell a whole story?

"Why didn't you call? You must've known the children would worry."

"I was half out of it."

"Sympathy pains in your other arm? Couldn't pick up the phone?"

"They gave me stuff for the pain." He fluttered his broken wing so I could see the cast. "Jesus, you've gotten hard."

"I had a good teacher."

"It's not becoming."

"Forgive me. We've had a little excitement of our own since you disappeared."

I wondered why I'd never noticed how close-set his eyes are. If he'd been involved in what had happened to Erica and Dot, would I see it in those eyes?

He leaned back in the chair and closed them, barring my glimpse into his soul. "The cops told me about Dot. Christ, what a nightmare!"

Dot's distorted dead face materialized. I struggled to exorcise her ghost.

"The police know you're back?"

"I've been to the precinct."

That surprised me. Had Ted Brodsky been there, I wondered if Rich would have walked out of that station so readily. The words popped out. "They didn't hold you?"

He sat up so quickly, the footrest flew back, striking his calf. "Ow! Fuck!" and glared at me as though I'd somehow engineered it. "Hold me? Why?"

"I just meant—it didn't look great, your disappearing when you did."

"Had to get away," he mumbled, rubbing his leg. "Going nuts, living in the house where it happened."

"Where were you?"

"Connecticut."

"Connecticut? What's in—"

"Cops told me you were the one found Dot."

"Yes."

"How was that? What were you doing in her apartment?"

Damned if I was going to let him put me on the defensive. "I went there looking for you."

"Why would I be there?"

"Come off it, Rich. I know about Dot. I know about all of them. I even know about you and Meg."

That was blowing the lid off.

He had the gall to look injured. "Again, me and Meg? You're crazy!"

I wanted to smack him across his lying mouth. I came around my desk and leaned over him. "I'm talking about when she modeled for you. Remember that? Because Brodsky knows all about it."

"About what, goddammit!?"

"About you and her, and her husband who's in jail, and Erica and the kickbacks—"

"Kickbacks!" He sprang out of the chair, grabbing my arm with his free one, hurting me. "What crap are you talking?" His voice became menacing. "I'm warning you, Carrie, if you've tried to make trouble for me—"

"Don't you threaten me!" the anger exploded up from the pit of my stomach and flew out of my mouth, engulfing me, engulfing *him.* I jerked away and pushed him back into the chair. "You hear me? Don't you ever threaten me again!"

He was stunned. This wasn't the old Carrie who had capitulated so easily under his killer lawyer's attack. *"You make trouble, you'll shoot yourself in the foot, lady. He's got the money, he's got the power!"*

He backed off. "I didn't mean—"

"Yes, you did, you bastard! You and that hatchetman you hired to do your dirty work. But it's over. Finished. You don't have power over me anymore."

He staggered to his feet. "I can't deal with you when you get emotional."

"When I stand up to you, you mean."

"Jesus, I came here to talk."

"There's nothing to say. Now get out of my office. I've got a patient coming."

As if to prove my point, there was a knock at the door.

"There she is. Good-bye, Rich."

Our eyes locked, but he was the first to drop his. With a shrug, he turned and opened the door—and came face to face with Ted Brodsky.

"MR. BURNHAM. I was hoping I'd find you here."

"I was just leaving."

"You won't mind giving me a few minutes of your time before you go running off again, will you."

It wasn't a question.

Rich shifted his weight, darted a nervous glance out the window as if hoping he could magically sprout wings and fly away. "Look, I've had a rough couple of days, and I'm not feeling a hundred percent right now."

"Yeah, sorry about your accident."

"I was on my way home."

"This won't take long." He indicated the recliner. "Grab a seat." I glanced nervously at the clock. Ten fifty-five. Phyllis Lutz was due any minute.

"Uh—Lieutenant, I have a patient at eleven."

"Looks like we'll have to do this at the station, then, Mr. Burnham."

"I was just there!"

"Sorry to put you out."

"Christ almighty, how many times do I have to go over the same thing!?"

Brodsky opened the door. "We've got two murders. Don't know what the killer's beef is, or if he or she might kill again. You knew both victims. From the looks of the Shea murder scene, it appears you might be in danger. Sorry, but you're an important link."

From behind Rich's back, he nodded at me. "Go right home after you finish here. I'll call you."

I PONDERED THAT in the few minutes before Phyllis was due to arrive. Why instructions to go right home? Did Brodsky want to keep tabs on me? Was I moving up on the suspect list again? I didn't think so. He must think I could be in danger. From whom? Rich? Erica and Dot were both connected to Rich, he'd made a point of saying that. Could that be the link? Rich had seemed shaken when I'd brought up the kickbacks and his relationship to Meg. But then, creating smoke screens had become an art form with him. Maybe Ted thought the danger might come from Meg. But why would Meg want to hurt me? I was no threat to her. Why hadn't she told me about her husband? About knowing Rich? Were all these players intertwined somehow? I shook my head, hoping the jumble of facts inside would fall into place, hoping to shake off my growing fear.

Phyllis was a no-show, so at eleven-thirty I took a lunch break. Odd, I thought. Her message had said she would call if she couldn't make it today, and Phyllis rarely misses an opportunity to bitch about her life, even if she has to pay for it.

From twelve to five I saw five more patients, doing my best to give them my best. I was inordinately grateful to Liz Brannigan who, when she picked up her son, Timmy, after his EEG training for his Attention Deficit Disorder, put her head around the door to tell me I was doing a terrific job.

I spent the next hour transcribing notes but quit when I noticed my hand trembling.

The skies were angry, and there were ominous rumblings in the distance as I left the office and dashed up Piermont Avenue to the market. Since both children were going to be away for the weekend, Allie performing with the chorus at a multischool concert in Boston, and Matt at his friend Jeff's country place in Putnam Valley, I'd decided to treat myself to a few gourmet items. Their plans had been made several weeks earlier, but the timing of the trips was God-sent. I was hoping the break would help restore their equilibrium and, possibly, their faith in their mother.

I was reaching for a can of pâté when I saw Phyllis Lutz, attired in golf uniform, down the aisle at the spices.

"Hey, Phyllis," I called out.

She turned, looked right through me, and pushed her cart in the opposite direction.

Maybe she hadn't seen me. I grabbed the pâté and hurried after her. "Phyllis, you missed your session. You okay?"

"Go away!" she hissed, not bothering to lower her voice. "Stop following me!"

My knees went weak. "What?"

"I should think I made myself clear when I blew you off today."

"Have I missed something? What's wrong?"

"What's wrong?" She reached into her cart and held up a copy of the *Phoenix.* "You're involved in a sordid murder case, for God's sake! Your husband's name's all over the papers. You're the latest Bobbitts. The town joke!"

There was a buzzing in my ears that I wasn't sure was coming from inside my own head or from the people who were beginning to stare.

I should have answered her. I should have annihilated her with some scathing remark. But my tongue was stuck to the roof of my mouth. I dropped the pâté and fled. From behind me I felt a hundred eyes boring into my back, a hundred tongues whispering and giggling.

The cab driver complained about the impending storm all the way home, while I sat in the backseat shaking with humiliation. Even the exorbitant tip I gave him failed to pacify. The minute I'd closed the car door, he roared off, spewing noxious fumes in my face and blanketing my shoes with dirt. Then the sky erupted. I stood on my front lawn and, together with the wilted daffodils, raised my face and let the rain revive me. I was drenched through by the time I let myself in the front door.

Except for the animals, tonight I had the house to myself.

Automatically I opened the back door for Horton and fed the cats while he did his business. Not as appreciative of the downpour as the daffodils, he was back nosing the cats away from their dinner before they'd had a chance to swallow. Placido and Lucie ran under the table, but José hissed and swatted him on the nose. He backed off. Small he may be, but José takes crap from nobody.

I opened a can for Horty, put his bowl on the floor, removed Lucie and Placido's dishes to the counter, watched as they leaped up and continued eating. The ritual used to drive Rich crazy, despite my scrubbing the counter afterward. One of the few advantages to divorce. You get to do your own thing.

I wandered to the fridge, hoping to find something to fill the hole in *my* stomach, settled on a semistale piece of Jarlsberg cheese and a couple of crackers. I poured a glass of wine, polished it off, poured another, went upstairs, and soaked in the bathtub while I gnawed at the cheese and drank the second glass of wine. Then I crawled out of the tub, wrapped myself in my old terrycloth robe, twisted a towel around my freshly washed hair, and lay down on my bed. I was just drifting off when the doorbell rang.

I jumped up, my heart pounding.

"Who it it?" I called from the top of the stairs.

"Ted Brodsky."

My hand went to my turbaned head. Well, nothing I

could do about the way I looked. I beat Horton to the door and opened it.

"Hi. Sorry to barge in on you like this." He was clutching his jacket collar tightly to prevent the rivulets dripping off his hair from running down his neck. I found his soggy state strangely appealing.

A sudden gust of wind showered us both.

"Think I could come in before I drown?"

"Oh, sure. Sorry." Embarrassed, I stepped back and watched as he carefully wiped his feet on the mat before stepping inside.

Horton gave a perfunctory sniff at the newcomer, then sat down and thumped his tail on the floor. Brodsky patted his head, was rewarded with a slurp on the hand. "Some watchdog."

"He hasn't lost faith in the human race yet."

"Well, he's one up on me." He mopped his face with a handkerchief.

"Take off your jacket. I'll get you a towel."

"How about I use the one you're wearing?"

I pulled it loose, foolishly pleased that my hair tumbled from under it, thick and wavy. "It's probably damp," I said.

"It'll do the job. Thanks."

He held out his sopping jacket. He was wearing a T-shirt, and jeans that fit. The damp jeans clung to his thighs, and I became acutely aware of his well-muscled legs, caught myself staring as he bent over to dry his hair, then, mortified, dragged my eyes away. Rattled, I hurried into the kitchen and spread the jacket carefully over the back of a chair.

Get hold of yourself! I scolded myself. *This guy is not a potential lover. He's a cop. Because you haven't had sex in nearly two years is no reason to behave like a bitch in heat. Just offer him coffee and find out why he's here.* "Lieutenant Brodsky," I called out, my voice carefully casual.

"Ted. We agreed it's Ted."

"Ted, would you like some coffee?"

He was behind me before I'd taken the can from the cabinet. "Sounds great."

I measured out the grains and plugged in the pot. When I turned around, he'd hung the wet towel over the back of the doorknob and was sitting by the table with José on his lap. José normally has to fight for his share of affection. He purred like a motorboat.

"You've made a friend for life."

"I see you have a set."

"Three, actually. We only planned to get one, but we couldn't bring ourselves to separate them."

"Sounds like you. What's his name?"

"José. After Carreras. You know, the tenor."

"Ah, then the other two have to be—"

"Luciano and Placido."

He smiled broadly. "What else."

Neither of us said anything until the percolator started perking. Not anxious to bring up the murders, I searched my mind for an innocuous topic, found it.

"Speaking of names, is it Edward?"

He looked up, puzzled. "Edward?"

"Your name."

"Oh." He made a face. "Theodore. My dad was a great

admirer of a couple of famous Theodores. Theodore Herzl, Theodore Roosevelt."

"Not bad role models."

He laughed. "I guess I can think of a worse philosophy for a cop than speaking softly and carrying a big stick. 'Course in today's society, it'd better be a thunder stick."

"I was named for my father's mother. Her name was Chaia. In Hebrew it means life."

"I know."

"You know?"

"I am that greatest of all anomalies—a Jewish cop. Son of Polish-Jewish immigrants. My parents met when they were kids—in Auschwitz."

I was stunned. "I'll have to tell Ruth-Ann. If she knew that, she wouldn't be so terrified of you. Are your parents still . . . ?"

"No." His expression hardened. "They managed to survive the camps, but not Brooklyn's muggers."

"I'm sorry."

He went on stroking José. I noted his easy manner with the cat, liked him for it. I couldn't be with a man who didn't like animals. Not that it mattered in this case, I told myself quickly, but it did make things more comfortable. Rich used to make a big deal about fur sticking to his pants.

I took two mugs from the cabinet and set them on the counter. Why didn't I just ask him why he was here? I filled the mugs, rummaged around in the turntable, and came up with a box of Oreos. "Cream and sugar?" I inquired with tea party formality.

"Black's fine."

He downed three cookies and the coffee and held out the mug for more. "You have an alarm system?"

Startled, I almost poured the coffee onto the table. "You think I need one?"

"At least you've got Man-eater here for protection."

"Horton," I corrected.

Hearing his name, Horton's tail thumped.

"Named after?"

"The elephant in *Horton Hears a Who*. Dr. Seuss," I amended when I saw he was at a loss. "You have to be a parent to get it."

"He trumpet or bark?"

"Barks. Often and loudly."

"Good."

I shifted uneasily. "You think I'm in danger?"

"Wish I knew. Haven't put the puzzle pieces together yet."

Somebody was worried about me. Somebody who wasn't paid to worry about me. Better. Somebody attractive, the first man I'd met since Rich who, let's face it, turned me on.

Healthy, I rationalized. *This is healthy. Doesn't mean you have to act on it. Just means you're alive.*

It popped out before I thought. "How come you never married?" Embarrassed, I added, "Of course, it's really none of my business, just most people by the time they hit forty or so . . ." My voice trailed off into the swirls of my coffee.

"Almost was." He put his mug down. "Didn't work out."

I let the quiet lie between us. Only José's steady engine broke the silence.

"I was with the NYPD. Shooting happened the week before our wedding."

I felt a coldness in my gut. I kept wanting to forget what went with being a cop.

"Pam came to the hospital, told me her nerves couldn't take it." He gave a half-smile, but it didn't make it to his eyes. "I'm sure you've heard about the divorce rate among cops. So it all worked out for the best, really."

I doubted he thought so. His wound was as raw as my own.

"Decided I needed a change," he concluded. "Job offer came along in Bergen County. I took it." He grinned. "So that's why you're stuck with me on this case. I really came over to bring you up to date. Your husband finally admitted he'd heard rumors about the kickbacks."

That phony. Acting like he'd never heard the word.

"The fight in the minister's study was more about that than the prenuptial."

"Why did he think Erica did it?"

"Like we figured. Power play. Punishing him for insisting on the agreement."

"Well, she was into power. And she didn't intend to end up like me."

"She didn't end up great."

"No."

"He agreed to take a lie detector test."

"Did he? Well, I don't think he'd do that if he had

something to hide." I remembered the boomerang. "You find any fingerprints at Dot's?"

"Some. Prints aren't on file with AFIS."

"What's that?"

"Automated Fingerprint Identification System. Computerized file of all known perps, plus whoever else might have been printed for job-related reasons. Picked up some of your husband's."

"Well, I guess he's spent a fair amount of time there."

"And there were yours. All over the place."

I shifted uncomfortably.

"Lucky for you they weren't on the murder weapon."

"You found the murder weapon?"

"Kitchen knife."

"What about the rock that Erica was hit with? You could compare the prints."

"Difficult to get a print off a rock."

"So it might not even be the same person."

"Possible. Not very probable."

I realized Ted Brodsky would never be discussing this case so openly with me unless he'd decided I wasn't involved. I began to feel like I could really get into this crime-solving business. So long as I didn't have to see any more dead bodies.

"You get out of Rich who he was with the past couple of days?"

"Gave us the name of a friend in Connecticut. We're checking it out."

"Man or woman?"

"Name of Marty Kramer. Attorney. Know him?"

"He does Rich's corporate stuff. But why would Rich go to his house? Why not see him in his office?"

"How good a friend is he?"

"They went to college together, but we never really socialized."

"Would Kramer cover for him?"

"I wouldn't think he'd stick his neck out too far. Did Rich tell you who the woman was at Haji's?"

"Said it was just a girl he'd picked up at the bar. Couldn't remember her name."

"I don't believe him." I grabbed his arm. "You know what? We should talk to Herb Golinko. He knows about Rich's women. You probably don't know him. He used to work for Rich until Erica made him quit."

He took my hand and held it between his. "I know all about it. He's dead, Carrie."

"What?"

"Golinko died this afternoon."

"Oh, God." Tears shot out of my eyes.

"I'm really sorry."

"He wasn't—?"

"No, no, it was the disease."

"I don't even know why I'm crying. He wasn't a close friend or anything. But he was a sweet guy, and he got a raw deal."

We sat for a while not talking. I didn't pull away until Horton got jealous and laid his head on my lap, wanting to be petted. Reluctantly I extricated my hand. Brodsky put José on the floor and stood. Reaching for his jacket, he said, "Want to go with me tomorrow?"

"Where?"

"Haji's. Bartenders have good memories."

"I'll be in my office till four."

"Pick you up at six."

"Okay."

"See you then."

When he'd gone, I mulled over why I'd agreed to go to Haji's with him, decided my reaction to him was normal. Coming off the rejection and pain of divorce, I'd probably have responded that way to almost any attractive man who paid attention to me. The trick was to recognize it for what it was, keep it in perspective. I'd seen this sort of thing often enough in my practice not to let myself be caught up in an inappropriate relationship.

Never married, I thought. Bad sign. Besides, he's a recovering dumpee, like me. His emotions can't be trusted. And remember, he's a cop. No sane woman would get involved with anyone who willingly walks into danger every day of his life. Whole thing's totally unworkable.

I went to bed, certain I'd come to the sensible conclusion. Still, I found myself looking forward to the following night.

Despite the constant drumbeat of the rain knocking against my window, plus having to contort my body around four sleeping animals, I got the best night's sleep I'd had since the whole bizarre sequence of events began.

SATURDAY
MAY 29

At FIVE-FORTY SATURDAY
evening, I was applying the finishing touches to my makeup when the doorbell rang.

"Who is it?" I sang out to show Ted how careful I was.

"Me."

Rich! Damn!

"If you've come to see the kids, they're not here."

"I came to see you. C'mon, Cat, open up."

Cat. Not Nudnik or Dragon Lady? I wanted to say "Go away!" I wanted to say "Go to hell!" But, don't ask me why, I opened the door.

The rain had continued on and off the entire day. Rich stood on the porch, a bedraggled pathetic figure, like one of those flood victims caught on camera watching his house float away. His face looked ravaged. His hair was plastered to his head, and his eyes were bloodshot with black rings under them as though he'd been drinking and hadn't slept. I felt zero desire to comfort him.

"Can I come in?"

I hesitated.

"Please."

I stepped aside, pushed the door shut against the wind. "What do you want, Rich?"

"To talk."

"We talked yesterday. There's nothing left to say."

"Please," he murmured again, heaving a sigh that should have moved mountains. "Would it be okay if we sat—maybe had a cup of coffee?" Not waiting for an answer, he walked into the kitchen and collapsed into a chair.

There was nothing I could do but follow. "Don't get comfortable. You're not staying."

I'd be damned if I was going to make him coffee.

"Just let me get dry." Picking up a paper napkin, he mopped at his face. "Don't suppose there's an old T-shirt of mine around here anywhere?"

"Only those I've cut up for rags." I walked to the sink

and tossed him a dish towel. "Why don't you go home and change?"

"Can't stand it there. Tried to sleep there last night. Nearly drove me crazy. So goddamned lonely."

Tell me about it.

When I didn't answer, he went on. "You can't imagine how empty that house feels without the kids."

I couldn't imagine that house at all without our children. "Our kids haven't lived in that house for over a year. Did you just notice?"

"It's hitting me how much I miss them. I keep listening for that awful loud music they were always playing, and those beeps from Matt's computer that went on half the night. All that stuff used to bother the hell out of me. Now all I hear is the silence." He leaned over and gave Horton's rump a couple of friendly smacks. "I even miss this elephant you call a dog."

He gazed at me expectantly. When the quiet became unbearable, he said, "Where are the kids, anyway?"

It annoyed me that he couldn't remember. "Allie went to Boston with the chorus. Matt was invited to Jeff's. It's why you have them next weekend. We told you about it."

"Oh, right. I forgot." He gave me the crooked grin that not so long ago would have had me on his lap, arms wound around his neck. "You look nice. Going somewhere?"

I glanced at my watch. "Very soon. Why're you here, Rich?"

"I told you. I wanted to see you."

I started toward the foyer. "Well, you've seen me."

He looked as though I'd struck him, started to get up, grimaced as his arm hit the table, sank back. "Christ!"

I softened. "You okay?"

He touched the arm gingerly. "It's killing me. And I'm starved. Haven't eaten a decent meal in days."

I didn't move.

"I can't believe what's going on. That fucking Brodsky grilled me yesterday like I was O.J. Where was I this day, that day—at three o'clock, at four o'clock, at ten o'clock? How the hell was I supposed to remember?"

"Try telling the truth."

"Dammit, Carrie, cut me a break."

Horton came over and sat next to me, his eyes shifting anxiously from one to the other of us.

"Rich, I really haven't got time—"

"Wait. Please. We're getting off on—I'm not doing this right." He rose, went over to the sink, poured himself a glass of water, drank. "You're making it hard." He fiddled with the folds of his sling, reached down, and rubbed his leg where the footrest had banged it yesterday afternoon. When he looked up, there were tears in his eyes. Matt's face, the time his baseball came through an open window and nailed my favorite lamp. "I know I haven't always been straight with you, but you have to believe me. I never wanted it to be bad between us."

The sociopathic mind is an amazing mechanism.

"Okay, I've been a bastard," he said, catching my reaction. "I put you through hell. Maybe it was the middle-age thing. Happens to lots of guys. But I'm over it." He crossed to where I was sitting, knelt, took my hand in his good one. "Cat, let's try again."

The words I had longed to hear. Why wasn't I dancing for joy?

He saw my hesitation, pounced on it. "You don't break a bond of nearly twenty years. I've learned that. There's still something between us. You know there is."

I did know it. No other man could be the father of my children. No other man would ever know the open, vulnerable young woman I had been—would ever share the memories constructed over a lifetime.

He read my mind. "We have so much history."

For a brief moment a picture of us as a family again played over in my head, and oh, how I would have given ten years of my life to have it the way it was—the way I'd thought it was. But then I remembered those terrible months after he left, for an instant relived the sleepless nights, the shock of going through his records and finding the paper trail of his betrayals.

He mistook my silence for capitulation. "I'll make it up to you. We'll be better than we ever were."

We. How long had it been since he and I had been a we? "What were we, Rich? Not what I thought we were."

He ignored that and went for my weak spot. "It'd be better for the kids. You know it would."

I looked at him then, searching his face for the man I'd loved, the man who'd cried with me when we'd had to put our old dog to sleep, who'd been there to help when my dad had his first heart attack, the man who'd lent me his strength when the doctor told us our first baby was in trouble and would have to be delivered by C-section. But there was no sign of him, only this stranger, this emotional cripple who could no longer give or receive love.

"You're not worried about Allie and Matt," I said wearily. "You're worried about you. Erica's gone, Dot's gone, you're tired and hungry and afraid of being alone."

"That's not true. I'm a man. Men make mistakes."

"A mistake? You really believe that's all this was?"

"I know it'll take time, but I've never stopped loving—"

My hand covered his mouth. "Don't say it."

I could hear the clock ticking, or was it my heart pounding? Sensing the tension, Horton slunk away from the table and curled up by the refrigerator, whining softly.

Rich struggled to his feet. "Well," he said in a last-ditch effort to salvage his pride, "I tried. Don't ever say I didn't try. Just remember the ball was in your court, and you threw it in my face."

"You'll be okay," I said softly as I followed him to the door.

"You bet I will. I don't need you or anybody."

"I know."

I watched him get in his Mercedes and roar off.

I wish I could say I felt elated, or at least a sense of satisfaction that I had once and for all cut the cord. I didn't. What I felt was lighter, as though I'd finally jettisoned a stone that had been pressing on my heart. Which is progress. The other, I guess, will come.

As I was closing the door, I saw a black car swing out of my neighbor's driveway and take off in the same direction. I tried to see the license plate but missed it. I decided I was getting paranoid about black cars.

WHEN THE DOORBELL rang fifteen minutes later, I found myself looking at Ted Brodsky with the eyes of a woman ready for a new relationship and fervently wishing we had met under different circumstances.

Sensing my mood, Ted tactfully refrained from asking questions. We made small talk while I searched for my raincoat, wedged in the back of the coat closet behind two snowsuits, a pair of skis, and the crutches Matt had used after his first trip to Hunter Mountain. I gave up trying to find an umbrella.

The rain had lightened to a fine mist. I stopped to admire the sleek white Miata parked at my curb.

"Yours?"

"Poor man's Porsche," he joked.

"It's beautiful. I thought the brown Chevy was yours."

"Department issue."

He opened the door for me, and I sank into the passenger seat. "Going to be interesting, watching you get in."

"Roomier than it looks." He maneuvered his long legs into the cramped space under the dashboard. " 'Course you have to be highly motivated."

The car slid smoothly into gear. Ted was a good driver. I'd imagined he would be. The other times I'd driven with him, I'd been too preoccupied with the catastrophe du jour to notice.

You can tell a lot about people by the way they handle

themselves behind a wheel. Ted drove at a good clip, as if he were one with the machine. Rich, too, had been a competent driver, except when he got pissed off at someone and decided to teach him a lesson by driving up his car's rear end. One night he flew out of the car and kicked a cab that had cut him off. It was the night of the snowbank incident. He broke his toe. Since then it's been a lot easier to believe in God.

Thoughts of Rich brought to mind the reason we were headed for Greenwich Village.

"If Rich is willing to take a lie detector test," I remarked as we crossed the George Washington Bridge, "you'll know if he was lying about the woman at Haji's."

"Maybe. The tests aren't always accurate."

I knew that was true from my own work teaching clients to bring down their electrodermal response levels. "I don't think he'd lie about her under oath. Unless they're both involved in some way."

"From what you tell me, your husband's a good liar."

"I was an easy sell. I would've believed him if he'd told me his mother was Anastasia and he was the czar's only surviving grandson."

"Don't go into the detective business. I wouldn't believe Anastasia was Anastasia if she showed me the crown jewels."

"Well, I'm savvier now. Did he tell you her name?"

"Sharon. Said he never asked her for her last name. They just talked and had a drink."

"Right. And they were playing catch with the pretzels."

"He denied that whole thing."

"You think she's important?"

"Right now everyone's important."

Traffic on the Henry Hudson moved at a steady pace in spite of the drizzle and despite its being Saturday night. We were in the Village in less than an hour from the time we left Norwood. It was getting dark by the time we made our way through the groups of Saturday-night revelers to the hazy smoke-filled café.

I could see this was primarily a singles' meeting place. Men and women, ranging in age from twenty to sixty, were standing at the bar three deep, eyes constantly on the move, checking out new prospects each time the door opened. I got a sinking feeling in the pit of my stomach at the thought that, one day, loneliness could drive me to a similar fate.

"It'll be a miracle if anyone remembers Rich and that woman," I whispered. "The turnover here must be mind-boggling. Isn't anybody afraid of AIDS?"

"It's a cold world out there. People're lonely," he replied with surprising compassion. "And they convince themselves AIDS only happens to somebody else."

His eyes swept the room. I wondered if he was trying to commit to memory that entire sea of faces.

An alluring young woman with heavily made-up dark brown eyes and long black tresses, wearing a revealing belly-dancer costume, led us to seats on huge green and gold cushions. She curled her lips in a sultry smile. "I'm Fatima," she said in pure Brooklynese. "I'll be your waitress for tonight."

Middle Eastern music wailed softly in the background.

Strange enticing aromas assailed my senses, making me aware I'd skipped lunch. In spite of our reason for being here, I began to enjoy myself. I hadn't been on a date since Rich left. Not that this was a real date, I reminded myself, but it was going to be fun sitting on the floor, eating food off a tray table.

I caught Ted's eyes following Fatima's swaying hips as she moved off.

"Watch it," I teased. "You're working."

"I'm a working stiff," he responded, a half-smile erasing the lines around his mouth. "Not a dead one."

MUCH LATER, AFTER we'd polished off a bottle of wine along with an assortment of Middle Eastern special-ties that we ate with our fingers, I got up to wash my hands, and Ted made his way to the bar. When I came out, he was deep in conversation with one of the bar-tenders. I went back to our table. Fatima was placing little cups of black muddy coffee on the tray.

"Everything okay?" she asked.

"Delicious," I replied. "Is it always this jumping?"

"Well, Saturday night, ya know, the singles're minglin'. It's quieter during the week."

I decided to prove Ted wrong about my detective skills. "You open for lunch?"

"Twelve to three."

"Long day for you."

"Yeah, but I only work Tuesdays, Thursdays, and Sat-urdays." She leaned over, displaying ample cleavage, and vacuumed the crumbs off the brass tray with a tiny hand-held brush. "And the tips're good. 'Specially after the show."

I'll bet they are. "You in it?"

She indicated the other waitresses. "We're all belly dancers. You should stay. The show's good. I'm good."

"What time's it start?"

"Eleven."

I saw Ted move away from the bar and begin a conversation with the maître d', who was all done up like a Turkish pasha, from his fez down to his elflike shoes.

"You ever have trouble?" I asked. "I mean, does it get rowdy?"

She made a face. "Well, sometimes you gotta peel the guys off you, but we got bouncers."

As she turned to go, I deliberately knocked over my coffee. "Oops, sorry."

Fatima whipped out a cloth from a hidden pocket in her voluminous pants. "I got it."

I moved Ted's cup out of the way of her quick hands. "Somebody told me you had some excitement here a few weeks ago," I said, as though making casual conversation. "Some woman making a scene, throwing pretzels at a guy. You see it?"

"Yeah," she hooted. "Yutz was givin' her a real hard time. She went ballistic. Let him have it right between the eyes. Management didn't like it much, but we was all cheerin' her on."

"You hear what the fight was about?"

"Man, I could write a book about the things go on in this place."

"What was she mad about?"

She hesitated, shot me a suspicious look. "What's it to you?"

"That yutz is my husband."

Instant compassion.

"Oh, jeez! God, I'm sorry. How long you married?"

"Eighteen years."

"Sonofabitch! You know how many of those creeps come in here hittin' on us? You could just puke!"

"What was the fight about?" I asked again.

Fatima gave me a conspiratorial grin. "You don't have to worry about that one anymore. I distinctly heard him tell her it was over."

I tried to sound pathetic. "What'd she look like?"

"You're much prettier, honey. The guy's an asshole." She shrugged. "But aren't they all!" And patting me sympathetically on the shoulder, she gathered up the coffee mess and glided toward the kitchen.

I closed my eyes, trying to shut out the noise around me, trying to assess what I'd heard. Was Rich picking women up in bars now? How long had it been going on? How could he take such chances?

With a jolt I realized Rich hadn't been exposing just himself to danger! *I* was one of those people Ted meant who thought it could only happen to someone else. God damn Rich to hell! How long was the incubation period for AIDS? Ten years, I'd read somewhere. I would have to be tested, and even then I couldn't be sure. By the time

Ted came back to the table, it was a miracle smoke wasn't pouring out of my ears.

"I understand how you feel," he said when I'd repeated Fatima's words, "but there's a silver lining to this cloud I don't think you've considered."

"Oh, right. Tell me how lucky I am he walked out before I definitely got something fatal." I was feeling hostile toward the entire male sex. I drained the remainder of my wine and picked up his glass.

Ted took it out of my hand. "Don't you see what this means? Given your husband's M.O., there're probably half a dozen women wouldn't have minded putting the competition in her grave." He grinned. "Bound to keep us cops busy chasing them down and off your case for a while."

I tried not to sound antagonistic—and not to slur my words. "You find out anything?"

He'd gotten pretty much the same story I had. Neither the bartender nor the maître d' had recognized the girl. She wasn't a regular. Rich was well known at Haji's. He came in from time to time, had a few drinks at the bar, and often left with some female in tow. No one remembered ever having seen this one before.

If Rich had been breaking off his relationship with her, obviously he knew her name. For some reason he was concealing it from the police. Why?

"Maybe she's from a well-known family," I conjectured, "and he's trying to avoid dragging her name through the papers."

"Chivalrous of him," Ted muttered disgustedly.

"Or it could be one of his models and he doesn't want gossip around the office."

"I'll have it out of him tomorrow," Ted said grimly. "Count on it."

I felt miserable. My head ached. I wished I hadn't started up with Fatima. Some detective I am, I thought. First time something throws me, I hit the bottle. Like Rich.

"Does he have an address book?"

I struggled to get my tongue around the words. "One of those Filofaxes. And a Rolodex." *Rolodex* came out "rodex." I tried again. "Ro-lo-dex. In his office."

"I mean a personal diary. Not something other people would have access to."

"If he does, he's never shown it to me. Which makes sense," I added darkly.

"Does he have a safe?"

"Not in the house. At least he didn't."

"In the office?"

"I don't think so."

"If he wanted to hide something where he'd have easy access, where do you think he'd put it?"

My mind wouldn't compute. *Keep this up*, I told myself, *you'll get to be one of those closet drinkers with a hidden stash.*

"Hidden bar!" I said.

"What?"

"Rich has a hidden bar in the office. It's in the wall. You push a button, and it swings open." I indicated the swinging motion and almost nailed the guy behind me. "I've never seen it," I told Ted excitedly, "but the kids know about it. If I wanted to hide something, that's where I'd put it!"

"Good girl!"

I grabbed his hand. "Let's go look."

He laughed. "Can't. Need a warrant."

"I don't. I'm still his wife."

"You're legally separated." He grew serious. "Don't do anything stupid, Carrie. We don't know where the danger's coming from."

"I'd be safe if you came with me."

"It'd be an illegal search. We'll wait for the warrant."

"But that could take—"

"I'll take care of it tomorrow. Promise you won't try it on your own! You forget what happened the last time?"

Dot's body floated in front of my eyes. "I promise."

He looked at the couples glued together on the dance floor. And took my hand. "Let's dance."

I pulled away, not wanting to deal with the signals my body was sending me. "I'll fall down."

"No, you won't." He drew me to my feet and led me onto the dance floor. "I won't let you."

And he didn't. We danced till two in the morning, only taking a break for the floor show. As she'd promised, Fatima was very good.

Ted was better.

S U N D A Y
MAY 30

TRIED TO KEEP MY PROMISE, I honestly did. I decided to clean the house. I vacuumed, mopped the kitchen floor, took out the garbage. I conjured up a mental image of a whisk broom and swept away the thought of that hidden bar each time it popped into my mind. I was doing great until I sprayed Windex on my beveled mirror in the front hall. The children's description surfaced. Beveled mirrors, Matt had said. Crystal stemware hanging from a wrought-iron rack attached to the ceiling. Dark oak cabinets and drawers containing a vast array of liquor. Allie had described a huge rectangular rack filled with wine and champagne. But the pièce de résistance, according to both of them, was a vibrantly colorful tapestry set in the center of the paneled wall unit, depicting frolicking peasants crushing grapes with their feet.

I wondered if the tapestry was there to conceal a safe. I wondered what stocks and bonds Rich might have secreted there, assuming it existed, concealed until some impersonal judge severed our bonds of matrimony, as though they were no more binding than the ribbon on a birthday package. And I wondered if one of those dark oak drawers contained files or personal records that Rich might have preferred to keep from Erica's prying eyes. And from Dot's. And mine.

You're being obsessive again, I told myself sternly. *Remember the trouble you got in last week obsessing over Rich and Erica's wedding!*

No use. Twenty minutes later I pulled into a parking space down the street from Rich's office building. The lot was empty, but I walked around the block before I got up the nerve to approach the front door.

Buildings that are meant to be bustling with activity have an eerie aura when they're empty. Footsteps echo off uncarpeted floors, every creak and groan seems magnified, signs of an unauthorized presence. I took the stairs two at a time, bolted past Dot's desk, uttering a silent prayer her computer wouldn't suddenly jump to life and type me a ghostly message, threw open and slammed shut behind me the door to Rich's office.

The room was dim, the only light spilling from behind the blinds, making zebra stripes across the white couch. It reminded me of the sofa in Dot's apartment. I stood panting for breath, afraid to draw attention to the room by opening the blinds or switching on the overhead. It took several minutes for my eyes to adjust. When they did, I moved around the room quickly, searching for anything that resembled a button or switch. I crawled under Rich's desk, figuring there might be a foot pedal, located one, pressed it in excited anticipation, and heard the door lock click.

My husband, the Boy Scout, always prepared.

I crawled back out, sat in Rich's twelve-hundred-dollar black leather, pneumatic-life, Chippendale-style executive swivel chair and ran the tips of my fingers under the rim of the desk. Nothing. I began moving objects on his desk, shifted the Lucite desk pad, peered under the lamp, flipped through the Rolodex, lifted the carved wooden pen from its ebony stand, and watched in awe, pen frozen between my fingers, as the wall opposite me split in two and swung slowly inward.

There it was in all its shimmering glory, crystal glass-ware reflected in the mirrors, wine bottles peeking out coyly from their cage, the tapestry just as Matt had described it—with one major exception. He had refrained from mentioning that some of the frolicking peasants, on break from grape-crushing, were stretched out on the soft green grass. Copulating.

Then I was out of the chair and inside the miniroom. No

safe lay concealed behind the explicit tapestry; a quick search of the drawers revealed no files. Frustrated, I peered inside the nearly empty refrigerator, tore apart the liquor cabinet, pulled out and replaced every bottle of wine. I threw open the dish cabinet and looked under every plate, noticed a book lying on its side on the top shelf. What kind of book would Rich keep in a bar? A recipe book for drinks, maybe? Doubtful. He took his liquor straight. Jumpy, pressed for time, I almost ignored the nagging voice in my head but, on a hunch, reached up and pulled the book off the shelf. It was a small book, burgundy with a navy blue binding. The title, *New American Poets*, surprised me. A gift, obviously. Unlike me, Rich wasn't fond of poetry. I started to shake it to see if anything would fall out, noticed a bookmark. I flipped to the page.

It's over, I read,
Bottle of gin balances precariously
on my kitchen table.
Unmade bed like some whale's rumpled
lost soul in my bedroom.
Ceiling fan whirring relentlessly above me,
lonely as an about-to-be-extinct bird.

He was in such a hurry he left
his running shoes standing pigeon-toed
in the closet, and his autumn-leaves-and-cologne
smell on the furniture, the bed
How much washing, airing out, before that's gone?

David Beckman's poem. It was familiar. Maybe I'd read it in one of the anthologies I keep in my office to clear my mind between patients. It works for my head the way sherbet between courses works for the palate. My eyes wandered to the last stanza.

> *No more brushing of his bulky body against*
> *me as we pass in the hallway, two animals*
> *sharing a warren, a lair, a cave.*
> *No more knowing laughs as we*
> *repeat old mantra-jokes.*
> *No more arguing like kids over*
> *which movie to see*
>
> *No more making up.* —
> *It's over.*

And, not part of the poem, in capital letters:
"*NO MORE PAIN! IT'S OVER.*"

Who had given this book to Rich? Which of his playthings? Had he even bothered to open it? Would the penciled-in words have disturbed him if he had? "No more pain. It's over," the woman had added. Like a woman contemplating suicide. Or—the thought burst into my brain like a rocket, billowing light. Or like a woman contemplating *murder!*

I could be holding in my two hands a very significant piece of evidence. I dropped the book as though it were made of molten lead, because if my deductions were correct, a killer's fingerprints could be on it. If they hadn't been smudged by Rich's as he opened it. Or by mine. Which I now realized, in growing panic, I had succeeded in plastering all over it!

BERATED MYSELF all the way home. Anyone with even a modicum of TV savvy knows no self-respecting burglar would dream of breaking and entering without wearing gloves. I knew the police had searched Rich's office after Erica's murder, but if Ted had the least reason to suspect anything, it would now be dusted for prints, and my fingerprints were all over the place. On the other hand, I reassured myself, if the police had reason to believe the killer might break into the office, surely they would not have left the building unguarded. Which brought to mind the possibility that I may have been spotted. Had there been an unobtrusive car or van parked nearby? Had I overlooked a road crew or a telephone repairman in the vicinity?

I knew Ted liked me—or at least that he found me attractive. I didn't think he'd revert to suspecting me of the murders just because I'd searched Rich's office. He knew what I'd been looking for. Still, he had to answer to his superiors. Who weren't attracted to me. And there was the matter of my broken promise. Somehow I didn't think that would sit well.

Now that I'd stolen the poetry book, what did I plan to do with it? If I couldn't tell Ted I'd found it, who could I tell? Meg would have been my first choice, but that was out of the question now. Why had I taken the damned thing anyway? I'd backed myself into a corner. I was in possession of illegally obtained evidence that might lead the police to the killer, and I'd tied my own hands!

A solution came to me, so simple I didn't know why I hadn't thought of it immediately. I'd call Rich and ask him who had given him the book. I'd have to tell him I'd been in his office, of course. And of course, he'd be ticked off, but this was about solving the murder of his intended. Once he realized that, he'd give the book to the police himself.

I stopped at a light and reached for the phone.

I never saw it coming, only heard and felt the crash. The car shuddered under me. Somehow I had the presence of mind to shove the gearshift into park, unsnap my seat belt, and throw myself onto the passenger seat. Instinctively I covered my head with my hands. In the distance I heard a screech of tires. When I looked up, the windshield had disintegrated into a crazy spiderweb pattern.

I don't know how long I lay there frozen in shock until a man appeared at the driver's-side window, waving a large rock. Terrified, I sat up and drew back.

"You all right?" he shouted through the glass.

I couldn't budge my vocal cords.

He knocked on the window and shouted at me again. "You hurt?" I felt the door shake as he tried to open it. "Lady, you okay?"

My mind was reeling. I couldn't think what to do. Why was this man trying to get into my car? Who was he? In a daze I managed to mouth *"I'm okay"* and wave him away. He looked disconcerted but took a few steps back.

"Black car, foreign job," he yelled, holding up the rock.

"Threw this right at you. Stay there! I'm gonna call the cops!"

Black car.

Paranoia set in. How did I know *he* hadn't thrown the rock? Maybe this was the killer! I had to get away. I realized the motor was still running and reached for the gearshift as I hit the accelerator. The car swerved wildly, almost veering out of control. I glanced through my rearview mirror, saw the man staring after me. Then he shrugged and tossed the rock into the gutter. And then I was shaking all over and crying, and I knew I was on the verge of hysteria.

Through a blur of tears and shattered glass, I tore into my street and pulled half over the lawn into the garage. I cut the engine and dashed toward the house. My fingers were blocks of wood as I tried to fit the key into the lock. Safely inside at last, I slammed and locked the door and dropped, exhausted, onto the couch.

The image of the splintered glass played over and over in my head. My skin went clammy just thinking what could have happened to me had I lost total control of the car.

Who would have deliberately thrown the rock? And why? Was it that man? Was he a hired thug? He'd mentioned a black car. Sue had mentioned a dark-colored car. Who owned a black car?

I took deep breaths until my heartbeat slowed, got up, poured a whole brandy glass of sake, had downed half of it before I caught myself. I was drinking too much. I was a person who worked with substance abusers, yet more and more I'd found myself trying to block out the horrors of the past week with alcohol. I put the glass down and focused on the situation.

Who had reason to want to harm me? Who knew my car? My habits? Who knew this neighborhood? Whom had I antagonized? Whom had I *rejected*?

Rich.

Impossible. Rich would never hurt me. Granted, with me out of the way, the children would live with him, he would retain all the assets of our marriage, and there would be no alimony payments. But he had loved me once, and I was the mother of his children. Besides, he'd agreed to a lie detector test. He wouldn't do that if he were guilty.

Unless he knew how to fool the lie detector. I had shown him how it's possible to slow one's electrodermal responses. "The "fight or flight" response. Wasn't that what a lie detector detected?

But Rich would have no possible motive to kill Erica.

Unless . . . it was a crime of passion. He'd returned home earlier than he'd let on, they'd had a fight, maybe she'd somehow found out about his cheating between the call I'd heard and the time he got home, and *she'd* dumped him! Or maybe she knew something related to the business that could sink the company and had threatened to use it. Rich was a wheeler-dealer. Maybe he'd made one bad deal too many.

My mind raced crazily on like a tape on fast forward.

As for Dot, she knew everything that went on in that office. She'd been furious when Rich had left me for Erica and not for her. Maybe she'd been blackmailing Rich. One thing I'd finally come to understand about this man.

Rich would sell Erica, Dot, me, and the children, with his mother and Horton thrown in for good measure, to save himself. The big question was, would he kill?

No! I concluded. Never. No matter what else he'd done, no matter how many other compromises he'd made with his conscience over the years, my husband was not a killer. I was as certain of that as I was of my love for my children.

I suppose there'll always be a piece of me that's connected to Rich. It's as though he were my left arm, turned gangrenous and necessarily amputated. I'm learning to live without the arm, but like the amputee, the ghost sensations of the strong healthy limb will stay with me for the rest of my days.

The appalling fact remained, however, that someone had tried to kill me today. I had no choice. I grabbed the phone and called Ted Brodsky. He wasn't at the precinct, would be back tomorrow, the impersonal voice told me. I left a message to have him call me immediately if he checked in.

I sat on the couch for a long time. Then I picked up the phone and dialed Meg.

SHE WAS AT my door in less than twenty minutes. She looked terrible, which in Meg's case just meant she looked beautifully sorrowful.

Horton didn't care what she looked like. He was all over her, licking her face and hands in delight as though it had been years instead of days since he'd last seen her.

She stopped to pet and hug him before turning questioning eyes on me.

I was the one who had made the call, but she had a lot of explaining to do before I was going to take her into my confidence.

"Why," I demanded icily, "didn't you tell me you knew Rich?"

"I couldn't, Carrie. You'd never've given our friendship a chance."

"That's a crock."

"It isn't. If I'd've told you, you'd have been out my door before the kettle had whistled."

My head was aching, and I didn't want to think about whistling teakettles. Horton started whining. It sounded to my ears more like Horton the elephant than Horton the dog. I grabbed for the doorknob.

"Out, Horty."

But the traitor just stood there frantically wagging his tail, gazing adoringly at Meg. Then he did something he hasn't done since he was a puppy. He lifted his leg and peed on the floor!

"Horty," I yelled.

"He's excited. Outside, Horty," Meg commanded, giving his rump a tap, and Benedict Horton trotted out.

It's a sad world when your own dog won't mistrust who you mistrust!

"I have a headache," I said, the understatement of the century, and headed for the kitchen and a roll of paper towels.

Meg followed. "You okay?"

"No."

"What's the matter? What's happened? Why'd you call me?"

First things first. "You lied about everything," I said, reaching for the aspirin bottle, struggling with the child-proof cap.

Meg, who has no children, took the bottle from me, gave a twist, and handed me two pills. "There's a difference between lying and not discussing something."

Oh, sure. I was familiar with lies of omission.

"When we met," she went on, "you were so broken up about Rich, I couldn't burden you with my problems."

My fault, right? I filled a glass with water, swallowed the pills, and grabbed the superabsorbent Bounty. "A whole year's gone by since then, Meg."

"Every time I decided to tell you, it seemed there was a new crisis in your life. Like now."

Who was I, Calamity Jane?

"I didn't think you could handle it."

I forgot all about Horty's accident, sat down overcome with guilt. Had I become so absorbed by my own problems that my best friend couldn't share her troubles with me? I didn't like the thought.

"Tell me now," I said.

"About who? My husband or Rich?"

"Start with your husband."

She pulled up a chair and lit a cigarette. "It was three years ago," she began, her voice so low, I could barely catch the words. "Kevin was president of a small pharmaceutical company. Peter, his brother, ran the animal facility. Pete's—well, he never really grew up. Their parents are dead, and Kev's always watched out for him. Anyway, Pete falsified some data on some scientific studies he never did. The drugs never went on the market because Kev found out about it in time. He was ready to kill Pete, but then the FDA investigated and Kevin reverted to being big brother. He covered for him. It was stupid."

"Where did you fit in? Brodsky told me—"

"I destroyed some letters from Peter that implicated Kev in the cover-up. That made me an unindicted co-conspirator." She squashed out the cigarette in a saucer. "Pete got probation and community service."

"And Kevin?"

"As president of the company, Kev was held responsible. He has three more months to serve."

What do you say to a story like that? "Sorry, I didn't have time to listen"?

"That's where you go, then," I managed finally. "On those days you disappear."

"I have to keep the café open on weekends, and there are no visiting hours on Tuesdays and Wednesdays. That leaves Mondays and Thursdays. If I've promised Kev I'll be there, I'm there." She took a breath. "I thought the trial was the worst experience of my life, but living without Kev is. It's one of the reasons our friendship's been so important to me. I didn't want to jeopardize it."

I was feeling pretty lousy about myself, but I wasn't finished with Meg yet. "Tell me about Rich," I said. "I know about the photo sessions."

"It was only two or three jobs, Carrie. A long time ago. Way before we met."

"Were you one of his little flings? Did you sleep with him?"

"No!"

I don't know why I said it. I hope it was the wine talking. "I don't believe you."

She looked at me a long time. "I can't help that."

She waited for me to say something. I looked away.

I heard the front door close behind her.

Horton came bounding into the kitchen, plopped down in front of me, and rested his head on my knee. I stroked his rough fur.

God did it right when he created dogs. If they love you, they love you for life. No trying to dig through lies and deceptions to figure out whether or not you deserve it. If you forget to feed them, they still love you. If you're mad at the world and take it out on them, they forgive you. We could learn a lot from the canine species.

Meg was backing out of the driveway by the time I got to the front door.

"Meg, wait a minute!"

She cut the engine and waited for me to reach the car.

"Please try to understand," I began haltingly. "After Rich, trust comes very hard. So when the facts were piling up against you, it was easy to believe I'd been taken in again." I concentrated on the door handle. "You paid for Rich. I'm sorry."

"Oh, Carrie."

And then she was out of the car, and we were hugging and laughing and crying at the same time.

Later, sitting at the kitchen table, I began telling her what had gone on the past couple of days. When I got to the part about searching Rich's office, her expression changed.

"When are you going to stop playing amateur sleuth? This isn't *Murder, She Wrote*. There's a killer out there! When are you—"

"Now! Right now. I'm not going to do another thing about finding the murderer. I swear. Okay?"

She was taken aback by my sudden change of heart. "Well, good. When did you decide to turn in your badge?"

"Today." I took a breath. "Come out to the garage. I want to show you something."

We walked outside. This is an old house, built in the days when a lot of houses weren't connected to the garages. Meg kept shooting nervous glances in my direction. Halfway to the garage, she stopped. "Christ almighty, Carrie, it's not another body, is it?"

"Not yet."

"What's that supposed to mean?"

I opened the garage door. "It means somebody meant there to be. But they missed."

The gasp Meg couldn't suppress echoed off the cement walls. "What happened?"

I blurted out the story. When I'd finished, she asked in a tight voice, "Have you called the police?"

"I tried to get Ted Brodsky. He was out of touch. I left a message for him to call me."

Meg approached the car. "A little more heave to that throw, and it would've ended up in your lap."

"I know."

"Do you?" Her voice was low, but I couldn't miss the underlying anger. "Do you understand what kind of danger you're in? Has it crossed your mind you could've been killed?"

"Stop it, Meg. I'm nervous enough."

"No, you're not! You're not nearly nervous enough! Goddammit, Carrie, you keep doing these crazy, foolhardy—" Tears suddenly sprang to her eyes and spilled over. "Let's get the hell out of here."

I grabbed the poetry book off the car seat and trailed her back to the house. I knew her reaction was born of concern for me, but it shocked me. I wasn't used to a Meg out of control.

At the front door she stopped. "That the book?"

I held it out. "Want to see it?"

"No, I don't. Just put it away somewhere till Brodsky gets here."

We closed and locked the door behind us. We were silent for several minutes, both of us breathing hard. Then Meg took my hand. "I have to get back to the shop. When are the kids getting home?"

"Late tonight."

"Do I have to stand over you to see you put in another call to Brodsky?"

"No. I was going to try him again."

"Double-lock the doors, and don't you dare go anywhere till I get here tomorrow. I'm moving in till this is over."

"I have a patient at nine, and then I promised the kids—"

"It's a holiday!"

She sounded like Matt, and I laughed, but it came out more like a croak. "I promise I'll be back by ten-thirty. You can come shopping with us."

"Jesus, Mary, and Joseph! You're too much!"

"Come on, Meg. Nothing's going to happen in broad daylight."

"Really? What about today?"

"I'll cab it over and back, I promise."

"Promises, promises," she groaned, throwing her arms around me. "You shouldn't be treating other people. You should be locked up yourself!"

"It would help if you came over and stayed with the kids while I'm out. After today I'd rather not leave them alone."

"Okay, I'll be here around eight. If you get home one minute after ten-thirty, I'm calling the police!"

After she left I hid the book on my bookshelf in among some other anthologies. I tried to watch some TV, but the strain of the day caught up with me. I lay down on the couch and was asleep in less than five minutes.

I dreamed Rich was running through the nature center in back of the house clutching the poetry book, and I was chasing after him, yelling, "Give me back my arm! Give me back my arm!"

MONDAY
MAY 31

THE FOLLOWING DAY WAS
Memorial Day Monday. There was no school, and I had
planned to take advantage of the sales and go shopping
with Allie. Matt was going to spend the day alternating
between Sam Goody's and CompUSA. Without a car
again we'd have to take a bus to the mall. I tried to think
how I was going to explain my shattered windshield.

I had scheduled only the one appointment. Vickie had left a message on my answering machine.

"Please, please, can I see you tomorrow? The Bloomingdale's interviewer set me up with an appointment for Tuesday morning with the Revlon rep. Can we work on a visualization to help me through it?"

I had called back, but it was telephone tag again. I got her machine, left a message saying I would make a special trip to the office and see her at nine. I wanted her to get that job.

I took a taxi and was in the office by eight-twenty, the only person in the building working on the holiday. I'd left the children sleeping. I'd forgotten to tell them I was going to the office, but Meg was there and would explain when they woke up. I figured they were exhausted from their weekend and would probably still be out cold by the time I got home anyway.

The heat wave had returned and held us firmly in its grip. I'd dug out an old cotton pantsuit, not caring that it was baggy and unironed, and slapped on some lipstick, deep-sixing my usual morning face-lift. Despite dressing for the tropics, I was sticking to my chair and my palms were sweaty as I reached for the phone to call Ted Brodsky. He wasn't in yet but was expected any minute. I left a message it was urgent I speak with him.

I pulled Vickie's chart and diskette, took out the prep gel and electrode paste, and switched on the computer. Glancing up at the wall clock, I saw I had half an hour till she was due, just enough time for me to do a quick alpha-theta session. Normally I try to rev up my creative juices by training for peak performance at least twice a week.

This week had been a disaster so far as my own brain-wave training was concerned. Maybe, I thought, if I go into a deep, meditative state, the pieces of this crazy puzzle will come together. At the very least going into a theta state would serve to quiet my overwrought brain.

Attaching the sensors to my head and ears, I checked the impedance meter to make sure I had a good contact, flipped my diskette into the computer, plugged in, and closed my eyes.

It was an effort to make my mind a blank. Images from the past week crowded my thoughts, thwarting my quest for stillness. Rich's sullen angry face Saturday night as he left my house, Matt's the day he'd fought for my honor, Ruth-Ann offering her cousin's karate-trained legs for the same reason. And sounds, the loud thumps of my own heartbeat after the rock smashed my windshield, thumps blocking out the chords of the software. And then . . .

I am inching across the swaying bridge, struggling to make it over the dark chasm to something—a shimmering opalescent bubble on the other side. Clutching the hemp rails, I move, step by driven step, past the halfway mark. My foot slips on the wet wooden slats, catches for a terrifying instant between them. I see the strands begin to fray, drop to my knees, crawl the final distance, and grab the ribbon dangling from the bubble as the bridge crashes into the watery abyss. And I am lifted high into the air, floating high over the water, safe at last. I look up—and in the bubble is Dot's dead face, and then it is Erica's, her elongated emerald earrings swaying in the wind, knocking against each other, swaying, knocking, knocking, bursting the bubble. . . .

Knocking. I FORCED my eyes to open, brought back to the present by loud raps on the door. I was shaken beyond anything I'd ever experienced in brain-wave training, by the strength of my abreaction and the knowledge that, until I faced my fears, I would be haunted by those images for the rest of my life.

With a sense of relief, I tore the sensors off, took a couple of minutes to collect myself, and buzzed Vickie in.

All dolled up in one of those lacy Laura Ashley dresses that made her look like the heroine of a gothic romance, she opened the door and peered at me from around the doorframe.

"Hi," I greeted her, making a gargantuan effort to cover my perturbation. "Come on in."

She didn't answer, just stood there posing against the frame, fussing with the flowing chiffon scarf at her neck.

Well, I thought, *good sign. She's in a modeling mode already.*

Looking past her, I saw Ruth-Ann come quietly up the stairs and take a seat in the waiting room.

Damn! What was she doing here? And then I remembered I'd forgotten to call her and tell her we weren't having Group this morning. I was about to get up and send her home when Vickie's expression caught my attention.

She was staring at me as though I'd suddenly meta-morphosed into a creature from another planet. Self-consciously, I smoothed my wrinkled blouse, wondering if my face showed the effects of the frightening visualization.

"Have a seat," I said, indicating the recliner. "We'll talk while I hook you up."

"How old're you?" she asked in her breathy voice.

"What?"

"I'll bet you're at least thirty-five or forty."

Great. Nothing I like better than starting my day with an abreaction followed by a discussion about a subject on which I'm becoming increasingly sensitive.

"Does my age have anything to do with why it was so important for you to see me today?"

"No. I just wondered."

"Good." I got up and reached for the prep gel. "Sit down and start relaxing and tell me about the interview."

"I guess you must've been pretty when you were young."

Okay, so some of us look better with makeup. "Thanks," I said wryly. "Now we've got that out of the way, can we—?"

"I'm a lot sexier, though."

I sighed. It was going to be a difficult session. "You want to tell me what this is about?"

"Why do you use the name Carlin?"

"Excuse me?"

"Your name's Burnham."

I managed a smile. "Carlin's my maiden name. I use it professionally because my degrees were earned when that was still my name." I indicated the framed diplomas hung behind my desk. "See?"

Her gaze wandered to the wall. "I only just found out about it."

"Well, it doesn't matter, does it? I'm the same person." I

indicated the recliner and switched on the tape recorder. "We still don't have any air conditioning. I know it's hot, but you have a lot you want to work on, so why don't we—"

"I don't think I'll be staying."

"What?"

"I won't be staying long," she repeated without budging from the doorway.

"You left a message saying you had to prepare for the interview with the Revlon rep."

She licked her lips. "That was just to get you here."

I blew. I couldn't help it. I was so uptight and so hot, my professionalism went flying out those useless windows. "Vickie, I've had a really difficult week, and I'm not in the mood for games. I came in especially on a holiday! I feel like I've been boiled in lava, and you come in here acting like—"

I stopped as all the saliva in my mouth dried up. Because Vickie's nervous fidgeting had tugged her scarf loose, and as I watched, it fluttered to the carpet like a wounded multicolored bird.

And I saw it—the antique gold pocket watch chain circling her delicate neck, its diamond and ruby clasp capturing the light from my lamp, the stones glittering and sparkling at the cleft in her throat like a hideous cluster of blood and tears.

The next thing I knew I was looking down the barrel of a gun.

"I'm really sorry," she whispered. "I like you, I really do, but you're Dickie's wife, so I have to send you off in a pink balloon just like the others."

A pink balloon. The visualization I'd given her!

Vickie and Dickie, Dickie and Vickie. The names boomeranged noisily off the walls inside my skull. Dickie was Rich! It wasn't that Rich had made one bad deal too many! He'd had one affair too many! And I was going to die because of it! Here in this hot hellhole of an office wearing no makeup and my ratty old pea-green pantsuit, my life was coming to an end!

"Funny it's working out this way," she said pleasantly. " 'Cause, you know, it all went down because of you."

Perspiration trickled down my face. Here I was in a real life-threatening situation; time for the adrenaline to start pumping, time for my fight or flight response to kick in! I cast desperately around for a weapon. I thought about the letter opener I keep in my top drawer, but there was no way I could get to it. My eyes lit on the impedance meter. It had weight. If I could just inch my hand toward it while keeping Vickie talking . . .

I forced my tongue to unstick from my palate. "What do you mean?" I croaked.

"You're the one told me to take charge of my life. You said I could make things happen instead of always letting them happen to me." She smiled brightly. "So I did."

I was afraid I knew the answer, but stalling for time, I asked anyway. "What things?"

"Remember when we did that exercise where you told me to put all the people who'd ever hurt me in a big pink balloon and send them floating away over the mountains?"

"It was a guided imagery exercise! You were only

supposed to do it figuratively—you know, in your imagination—to help you deal with getting them out of your life."

"I know, but I thought how much better if I could get rid of them for real." She giggled. "So I sort of—you could say, stuck a pin in the balloon." She made it sound as if she were a naughty girl who had played an innocuous prank.

My hand crept toward the meter. "You didn't even know Erica and Dot. How could they have—"

"Dickie was going to marry Erica. And Dot wanted him. She found the pictures he took of me, and she called me up. She invited me to her apartment, but I went earlier than she said. I surprised her in the bathtub. She wouldn't give them to me. I had to find them myself."

"But why did you have to—why did you—"

"She guessed about Erica. She was going to turn me in so she could have Dickie. She had pictures of him all over her walls, you know," she went on conversationally, "like he was hers. I didn't like her having all those pictures, so I tore them up.

"Vickie," I pleaded, "I've never hurt you. I don't deserve to be sent off in a pink balloon."

"I know," she said, lowering the gun. "This makes me really sad. But Dickie wants you back. Only 'cause of the children probably, because I'm much younger and prettier than you."

"No! He doesn't—" I started to protest.

"I saw him go in your house. He wants his children." The gun came up again, pointing straight at my heart. "But you won't be lonely for long. 'Cause after we're married, I'll send the children to you."

My heart stopped beating. Then cold rage replaced terror. No way was I going to let my children, my beautiful Allie and my sweet Mattie, die at the hands of this psycho!

My fingers crept the final millimeters and closed over the cold metal box. I glanced up, measuring the distance I'd have to throw it to knock the gun out of Vickie's hand.

And then I thought of Ruth-Ann. From her chair she could see only Vickie's back, so I knew she was unaware of what was happening.

How could I communicate the danger? If I yelled at Vickie to drop the gun, she might shoot me *and* Ruth-Ann.

"What kind of car do you drive?" I asked loudly, my voice trembling.

"A Camry. Why?"

"One of those Japanese cars," Sue had said. *"A foreign job, black"* from the man with the rock.

"Because when you threw that rock at my car yesterday, a man saw you, and he described your car. It's black, isn't it?"

The gun wavered.

"He also got the license plate number," I went on, "so the police know who you are. They know you killed Erica and Dot."

Ruth-Ann was on her feet now. I sent her a silent screaming appeal. *Call 911, Ruth-Ann! Get out of here and call 911!*

But my mental telepathy mechanism was on the blink. She didn't get my message. I saw her reach into her bag and pull something out.

Oh, please, let it be a gun, I prayed, though I couldn't picture Ruth-Ann carrying a gun.

A sly smile played over Vickie's face. "You're just saying that to scare me."

I continued talking loudly so she wouldn't hear Ruth-Ann. "Have I ever lied to you?"

I flinched as the gun bobbled in her hand. "No."

"I'm your therapist. You need me. I can make the police understand that you—you're—confused. . . ."

Wrong approach. I heard the safety catch click off. "I'm not confused!"

"You're confused about Rich—Dickie. He doesn't want me. He only came over last night to talk about visitation rights because we're getting divorced."

Then I saw what Ruth-Ann held in her hand. Her car keys! *Car keys?* What the hell did she think she was going to do with—

And then things happened fast. Ruth-Ann's hand came around in front of Vickie's face, spraying something. I ducked as Vickie screamed, clawing at her eyes. The gun went off, but I seemed to be alive, so I threw the meter with all my might straight at her. And missed! The gun was waving around wildly. I dashed around my desk, grabbed her flailing arm, smashed her hand against the desk, shaking the gun free. I heard it bounce off the wall and saw Ruth-Ann kick it away. Blinded, howling, thrashing violently, Vickie fell to the floor. Her long arms reached out, found my leg, pulled me down on top of her, her graceful body infused with the strength of a wildcat. I felt her teeth sink into my arm, my cry of pain cut short as her legs wrapped around me like a boa constrictor, squeezing the breath out of me. Then Ruth-Ann was pulling them off, and I heard Vickie give a yelp as, from out of my tearing eyes, I saw Ruth-Ann plop her plump little body down on Vickie's legs, pinning them firmly to the floor.

As sweet air filled my lungs, a blind hot fury took hold of me. My hands were on Vickie's throat, and I think I was banging her head on the floor, and then two strong hands were prying my hands loose, and Ted's arms were lifting me, pinning me to him, and I could feel the comforting roughness of his jacket against my face, and his voice was murmuring softly, calmly, "Stop, Carrie! Let her go. Stop. It's over. You did it. You got her. It's over."

EPILOGUE

WEDNESDAY
JUNE 2

"*I LIKE YOU, I REALLY DO. But you're Dickie's wife, so I have to send you off in a pink balloon just like the others. . . .*"

Vickie's childish voice invaded the room as I stood by my desk and played and replayed the tape. I couldn't believe she had taken my innocent suggestion about a harmless way to deal with her destructive feelings and turned it into something deadly.

I rewound the tape, hit the play button.

". . . *you're Dickie's wife, so I have to send you off in a pink balloon just like the others.*"

I sank into my chair, buried my face in my hands. "How could I have missed how sick she is?" I moaned aloud.

"You want to blame someone, Carrie, blame her psychiatrist. Or better yet, blame your husband." Ted materialized in the doorway. He walked into the room and hit the stop switch.

"I should have seen it," I whispered.

"No one saw how crazed with jealousy she was. You stopped the slaughter."

Strange how just the sound of his voice made me feel better.

"How'd you know to come?"

"Your husband finally gave me Vickie Thorenson's name. She was the girl at Haji's. He'd been trying to keep her out of it. Embarrassed, I suppose, to have it get out he'd been fooling around with a teenager."

Funny how that part of it hadn't struck me. Vickie would have been celebrating her first birthday the year Rich and I celebrated our wedding.

"One of my very efficient detectives remembered seeing it on your patient roster," Ted continued. "Coupled with your messages and a message from Meg about the attack on you and telling me you were alone in your office—" He touched the bandage on my arm. "I thought I'd better move my ass."

"Thank God for Ruth-Ann. If she hadn't shown up and had that pepper gas in her bag . . ." I shuddered.

"Pepper gas's illegal in New York, you know." Ted's voice was solemn. "Might have to arrest her."

My eyes flew to his face. "Oh, right, just like a cop! I could've been killed!"

He was laughing. "Just kidding. They changed the law. But I'd've been lenient."

"Big of you."

"Who would've thought that shy, ultrareligious little girl would be packing Mace?" he mused.

I knew why. Ruth-Ann had been raped. *"People like us— we have to fight back,"* she'd said. *"Tell them never again."*

"She told me she loves you. You'd saved her life, and she would've done anything for you."

"She almost gave her life for me." It was a sobering thought.

He reached out and touched my cheek. "You must give a lot of love, to inspire that."

"Funny. For so much of the past year and a half, I've been filled with a very different emotion," I said softly. "I hated Erica. You don't know how often I imagined killing her myself."

"The green-eyed monster's inside all of us. Difference between us and the Vickies of the world is, we keep our monsters caged." His hand rested lightly on my hair. "Let's get out of here. Feel like some lunch?"

I rose and gave him a shaky smile. "Okay."

"How about dinner Saturday night?"

We walked to the door, and I flipped off the light, closing the door behind us. "You asking me out on a date?"

"Sounds like it."

"Haji's?"

"That's for people still looking." He pulled me to him. "I know a terrific little restaurant right here in Piermont—soft music, dim lights, great food. Kind of place couples go."

Something stirred inside me then, a warmth, a letting go, something I hadn't felt in a very, very long time. I tried to identify the emotion, and slowly, it came to me. I think it was what I used to call—feeling happy.